To Nancy,
Reg wanted you to have
some entertainment while you
and your butterflies were
driving those big trucks.
Enjoy!

Jean C. Keating

Bev. Abbott

Pawprints
On My Heart

Edited by

Jean C. Keating

Illustrated by

Beverly S. Abbott

Astra Publishers

Williamsburg, Virginia

Library of Congress Catalog Card Number: pending
ISBN # 0-9674016-1-5

Printing November 2000
10 9 8 7 6 5 4 3 2 1

Front Cover: *Papillon Family* by Bev Abbott
Back Cover: *Paw Prints In Snow* by Bev Abbott
Astra logo by Beverly S. Abbott, For Arts Sake

Web design and hosting by Virginia Networks: rdennis@richmond.net

Copies available from the publisher:

Astra Publications
209 Matoaka Court
Williamsburg, VA 23185
(757) 220-3385
www.astrapublishers.com

ACKNOWLEDGMENTS

Dot A. Bryant deserves a large measure of credit for the editing of this book. She has persevered through all the many versions of the illustrations and layouts to produce the beautiful manuscript from which the book was printed.

Thanks also go to Alan MacDonald for the beautiful tribute to Miss Bris that appears on page 94 as a part of this wonderful dog's story.

Books from Astra Publishers

Amorous Accident: A Dog's Eye View of Murder by
Jean C. Keating

Mercy Me by John Atkinson

DEDICATED TO

Ira H. A. Abbott

..... who spent endless hours merging text and illustrations to make this book possible.......

Table of Contents

List of Illustrations

Pawprints
On My Heart

Introduction
by Jean C. Keating

They give so much, and ask so little, these companions in fur. They offer uncompromising love, the warmth of total acceptance. They live in the moment, expressing their joy at our company with unabashed devotion. They teach us, when we let them, to enjoy the here and now. They comfort when we are distressed and are joyful at our happiness. They need us, give us focus, give us a reason to go on. During their all too brief passage through our lives, they leave paw prints on clothes and carpets, on hearth and home. Even when their earthly journey is over, the memories of their pranks, companionship, and love enrich our lives as long as memories exist. May there always be Pawprints On My Heart.

Joyce A. Davis

Although she was born in Wilmington and graduated from the University of Delaware, Joyce A. Davis has lived most of her adult life in Tidewater Virginia. (Norfolk, Virginia Beach, Hampton, and now, Gloucester.) Joyce, her husband Hugh and their Lab-mix, Dixie, live on 18 wooded acres in Gloucester, adjacent to a large tree farm where they enjoy taking long walks. For eight years, Joyce wrote a weekly humour column for the Petersburg *Progress Index*. Her work has also appeared in the Newport News *Daily Press*, the York *Town Crier*, and several weekly and monthly newspapers and magazines. She is currently writing a column for *Chesapeake Style* magazine and working on a novel. Joyce and Hugh have two married children and three grandchildren.

Pink Lady Pandemonium
by Joyce A. Davis

It was awful. In fact, it was the worst day of my life.

All I wanted to do was take my dog to the vet for a routine shot, but it was Saturday and the waiting room was jammed. There were people with all kinds of animals-- dogs, cats, a hamster, a squirrel, and even a parrot in a cage. It was hot and stuffy, and I was struggling to keep my nervous German shepherd from taking a bite out of one of the other dogs.

Then in came this woman carrying a Siamese cat. She wore a pink dress, a pink hat, pink shoes, and carried a pink purse under her arm. Her stilty, bird-like legs made her look like a flamingo.

"Ooooh, look, Toodleums," she cooed to her cat. "Look at the mansey-wamsey with the itty-bitty hamstey-wamstey." She bent down so her cat could see into the cage. "Bet you'd like to get your itty-bitty pawsie-wawsies in there and catch the hamstey-wamstey, wouldn't you, Toodleums?" she drooled. The hamster's owner was not amused.

From there the pink lady went to the parrot cage. "Ooooh, look, Toodleums. See the big big birdie." She caressed her cat. "That birdie is too big for Toodleums to play with. He might scwatch you." Toodleums gave the parrot a cross-eyed stare.

Then the pink lady went to the man holding a papillon. "Ooooh, look at the itty bitty pommie-wommie with the big ears," she said. "Isn't he fweet? Does Toodleums want to kiss the itty-bitty pommie-wommie?" She bent down so her cat could get a closer look.

"He isn't a pom, lady. He's a papillon." The dog's owner glared; the papillon reached a paw out to push the cat away.

From the "pommie-wommie" she and Toodleums went to the "Squirelly-worley." Then I could see she was headed my way.

"Ooooh, look at the big doggie-woggie. My Toodleums would love to have you for a fwend, wouldn't you, Toodleums?"

"No, please, no," I protested, trying to get a grip on my dog's collar. "My dog doesn't like cats. They excite him, and there's no telling what he might do."

The pink bird ignored me. "Oh, we don't beweave you. My Toodleums knows a fweet doggie when she sees one."

I did what I could to keep the bird with the cat away

from my dog, but it was no use. My pet broke loose, sniffed the lady's legs, then lifted one of his. Ms. Babytalk shrieked and Toodleums jumped out of her arms, landing on my dog's back. From there the cat went to the top of the parrot cage, knocking it to the floor and releasing the parrot, who flew to the light fixture on the ceiling and cussed everybody out. The parrot cage rolled over and tripped the vet, who was just coming through the door, causing him to sprain his ankle.

In the melee that followed, the air was filled with fur, feathers, shrieks, and the whine of an ambulance. Ms Babytalk fainted, the doctor was in pain, and they'll *never* see yours truly on a Saturday again.

Why You Shouldn't Own a Dog or a Cat
by a Dog and a Cat
(as told to Joyce A. Davis)

My dog, Lucky, looked at me with disgust. "There's something I've always wanted to know," he said. "Why do you keep four cats? Take Tabby over there--look at her. She's got more stripes than a jailbird. Little moth-eaten flea bag. Little hairball. Someday when you're not looking I'm gonna get her. And those three friends of hers, too--bunch of squirrels. What a con game they've pulled. They meowed their way into this house and took over. Me, at least, you went looking for.

"You think you've got 'haints' in the night, what with stuff flying off the tables and all? What you've got is a passel of cats carousing around like a bunch of drunks at 2 a.m. They create enough racket to make a dead man cry. You don't see *me* nibbling the leaves off your house plants, do you? Wanna know what happened to that vine your Aunt Mary gave you? Guess.

"Fair weather friends, I call them. As long as you dish out the food they're loyal. You come home and I greet you at the door. They look up and say, 'What? You again?' You might as well keep a bunch of three-toed sloths around the place.

"Just the other day I saw Feisty knock over a glass of milk and then step in it. You should have seen her prissy her way out of that--shaking her dainty paws. Thank heaven *I'm* not squeamish. And you don't see *me* falling out of second story windows, do you? Or getting stuck behind the wall, or inside the linen closet? You don't see *me* getting trapped in an old washing machine. Or hiding in the wheels of an airplane. You don't need a cat."

Tabby jumped on my lap and pierced me with her green marble eyes. "I heard that," she said. "and you don't need *him*. Why do you keep that flop-eared slobber-mouthed thing around anyway? You don't see *us* hanging our heads out of car windows with a big tongue flapping in the breeze. He says we eat house plants? You ought to see some of the things *he* eats.

"You hear a siren and he howls. He howls when you play the piano too, don't he? And remember *he* was the one who got his head stuck in the fence that time and you had to call the rescue squad to get him out. Embarrassed you, didn't he?

"And last week, didn't he stick his nose in where it didn't belong? You had to pour four cans of tomato juice over him and he *still* reeks of skunk. *We* at least have some dignity.

"Lucky thinks we cat around? You ought to see the cheap crowd he travels with whenever he gets out at night--bunch of junk yard riff-raff running all over the place.

"We cats have been civilized since the pyramids were built. We were *worshipped*. Considered *sacred* when dogs were nothing but hang-arounds. As social assets, they're failures. Always wagging up to people, swishing their whole bodies back and forth and licking people in the face. Cats don't come to people. People come to us. I'd as soon have a raccoon as have a dog around this place. They're outlawed in Iceland, and they should be here, too."

I looked down at my two favorite pets, scratched Lucky's ear and stroked Tabby's head. Then I gave them my answer.

"I don't need a dog?
I don't need a cat?
No Lucky at my feet?
No Tabby on my lap?
Life would be so lonely
Without friends like that.
I'll *always* need a dog.
I'll *always* need a cat."

Page 9

Beverly S. Abbott

Born in North Carolina, Bev Abbott has lived on the Virginia Peninsula for most of her life. She has always drawn and created her first oil painting depicting a swan at the age of twelve. Her ambition in life from an early age has always been to be an artist. Along the way, she reared two children and countless dachshunds with the support of her husband Ira.

Together they travel the country in a 35' motor home in search of soft adventure, seeking inspiration for future oil paintings. She grounds her art in accuracy but designs with creativity and imagination, just like her writing. The grizzly bear story is the result of one such adventure. The wild free-roaming bear really was within three feet of her toes. Leo was her first dachshund love in 1972 and Annie is her current love bug.

She has owned, loved, and been controlled by her miniature dachshunds for 28 years. She began painting all breeds of dogs in 1979. Painting top show dogs and creating trophies for national dog clubs was her focus for many years.

Earth Bound Cloud
by Beverly S. Abbott

Swirling, whirling mass of white, floating here and there.
Under my feet,
between my legs like powdery windblown snow.
Sparkling, teasing, tickling bubbles of champagne.
Leaping, twirling, spiraling fluff of feathers flying.
Sprightly tiny pirouettes curling toward the stars.
Yips and yaps, airy and billowing,
swell and flow around me.
Stretching to caress,
the surreal mass fades and dances away.
Cold noses, warm wet tongues greet me with buoyant joy.
Slowly, gradually the frantic leaping begins to calm.
Then do I detect the contents of the twisting wispy froth.
Earth bound cloud becomes fourteen joyful Papillons.

Trust the Nose
by Beverly S. Abbott

"Leo, my mighty backyard hunter and tracker, I want to see how good you are in the woods. Into your crate you go," said I, the human partner of this team. "You get to go also, Joy." I watch Leo's little Dachshund tail wag in a very fast figure eight. He gives this unusual little twisting action to his tail whenever his excitement reaches a high peak. Crate time means an adventure for these two Miniature Dachshunds. My dogs relish fun, games, and new smells. Leo enjoys tracking Joy (his kennel mate), squirrels, moles, cats, and any wild critters that may come into his yard.

Excitement mounts also with me as I enjoy walking in the woods at my father's Spring Landing Hunt Club on a warm spring day. After an hour's ride we arrive at the turnoff to the narrow rutted dirt lane leading through the woods to the cabin. This road, barely more than a wide path, has two deep ruts with grass growing between them. Small wild critters dart across as we approach.

Leo and Joy are both barking now as the smell of the pine trees and wild scents invade the car.

"Hi, Daddy", I said, as we all piled out of the car: Leo, Joy, human food, dog food, crates, leashes, bowls, and water. I cannot seem to travel light. Daddy, laughing, says, "Where is the kitchen sink?"

After settling down and finding a place to put everything, I leave Joy in her crate on the porch of the cabin. With loud barking, she lets me know she does not approve of the arrangement. Daddy and I, with Leo in the lead, marching with head held high, start down the dirt road on foot. At the point where a footpath takes off through the woods, we turn right and follow the path. The sun shines bright and warm. The breeze blows, fragrant with the smell of wildflowers in bloom. The trees grow greener by the minute. "Idyllic day" comes to my mind.

Along the footpath the undergrowth becomes thicker. Leo's nose glues itself to the ground. With deep concentration and a madly wagging tail, he follows the scent of countless squirrels that have scurried by. He stops to paw at a spot then becomes distracted by an even more enticing odor. We humans are just ambling along enjoying the company.

Leo's hunting takes him further away from the trail, as the smells are so enticing. Leo, poking his nose under leaves and down holes, looks to see if anyone is home.

Trust the Nose

Coming to a rotting log, he sniffs along its length to a burrowed out hollow under the old root system. Leo finds himself nose to nose with a critter who seems to be very cross at being awakened during the day. Out it pops, snarling and stamping its feet. The black and white striped musky animal is very unfriendly. The little red and black dog decides to leave the little black and white critter alone and move to other trees.

The leaves and debris on the ground hold more enticing scents encouraging Leo along the trail. Walking around an old oak tree, he sees an animal about his size but with a very sharp nose and even sharper pointed teeth. She has a long hairless tail and many little babies clinging to her back. Snarling and hissing, she shows how angry and frightened she is by the intruder. She has her large family to protect.

Again, Leo decides to move on. Spotting a bushy tail, Leo gives a yip of joy. With ears flying in the breeze, his little body folding up and stretching out like an accordion, he takes off after the squirrel. The squirrel realizing something is after him dashes up a large oak tree. From the safety of his high perch, he turns to see his adversary. Chattering and barking angrily, he begins to drop acorns down on Leo. Ping, one hits him on the head. Leo barks back. Soon a blue jay swoops in to add to the din with his raucous calls. The entire racket has disturbed a sleepy owl that begins to hoot. The jay dives low over Leo several times. Leo finds the woods belong to the creatures that live there and decides to return to his people who want him around. Following the trail of his own scent Leo makes his way back to the dirt road which leads him back to the cabin and Joy in her cage.

Suddenly I stop, realizing I have lost sight of Leo. Being so low to the ground, he can easily disappear into the underbrush. Daddy and I begin to call, "Leo, Leo, here Leo, Come, boy." No response. I start to panic. Leo is so little and has never been in the woods before. Since Daddy knows the area well he says, "I'll walk in this area down toward the river." As I wait for his return, my panic becomes stronger. Off in the distance I hear the noise of the forest creatures. A squirrel chatters, a blue jay calls excitedly and an owl hoots softly. After what seems to be a long time, Daddy reappears. "I did not find Leo but I did find this pretty wildflower." Hoping to make me feel a bit better, he hands me a Purple Gentian wildflower that he found down toward the river. It has the appearance of tiny purple candelabra. As a small child whenever I asked my father, "What is your favorite color?" He would always answer, "Burple" which I took to mean purple and would correct him. He would then insist the color was burple. The color has special connotations between us. The flowers are just his way of showing his concern for me and trying to ease my fears for Leo's safety.

By this time, we could hear Joy barking impatiently back at the cabin. We are not far from it as the crow flies. We start retracing our steps calling Leo as we go. Worry hangs about me like a dark shroud.

I can see the cabin, as we walk around the bend in the road, with Joy barking from her crate. Beside her sits Leo with a mischievous grin on his face. It appears Leo, following his own scent, has retraced his steps back to the dirt road.

Additional members of the hunt club returning from a trip into the nearby village for work supplies tell me what had transpired. With much amusement, one tells me, "we were driving the truck up the dirt road when Leo burst out of the woods in front of us. He led the way, down the middle of the road, all the way back to the cabin, his head

Trust the Nose

held high like a band master leading a parade."

Feeling foolish for not trusting his nose, I wipe a spider's web and leaf debris from his head and give Leo a big hug and a good lunch. His tail wags a vigorous figure eight. Whether his excitement comes from finding me or lunch cannot be determined.

Annie and the Grizzly

by Artistic Antics (Annie) as told to Beverly S. Abbott

How do I manage to get myself into such predicaments? Is it because I am a sweet innocent little Dachshund lady and never cause any trouble? Well! At least I don't think I cause any trouble! My person does that quite well herself, when she brings me on her nature trips. She calls the trips "gathering resource material." Personally, I think she just uses that as an excuse to go traveling. She peers through a small box that makes strange clicking and whirling sounds. I enjoy the petting, ear scratching, and tummy rubs I receive from the other humans we meet on the trails. I bark most vigorously at the strange smelling wild critters we see on these long trips. I must warn them to make a wide detour around my person. She is so trusting. Why, she will walk right up close to all kinds of strange creatures, from snakes to bison, with that box in front of her face. She has no fear, as though all animals are as sweet as I am or else she thinks that is a magic box she holds in her hands, that will protect us. I must take responsibility for the two of us. Being of the four-legged variety myself, I know best how to deal with the wild critters.

Sometimes, I have watched her stare off into a distant space moving the box this way and that before it makes a clicking sound. There are only open fields and distant mountains in front of us. It is at these times that I worry the most about her intelligence. There is nothing to look at that I can see. She announces that will be a good picture with a look of satisfaction on her face. Then we move on to look for another scenic place that she has in mind. She seeks out those animals she calls eagle, coyote, elk, moose, and big horn sheep. Every time, I start a barking frenzy to warn her of the danger. Usually, she yells at me for scaring off the animals instead of rewarding me. Becoming indignant, I stalk off in a huff when my protective services are not appreciated.

We have been on this trip for a long time. I have heard the name of Alaska several times. I will admit it is beautiful here! The smells are exotic and fascinating. Today we are in Hyder, Alaska along a creek that is just swarming with things that are longer than I am. She calls them salmon. The salmon swarm like bees in the swift running icy cold creek. The glacier about a mile upstream melts just enough during the summer to create the ideal conditions for the salmon to spawn. Thousands of them swim by, packed together like sardines in a can.

My person has set up her oil painting easel along the bank of the creek. She begins to paint a picture of the small calm pond that branches off to the side of the creek. With a silly happy grin on her face, she stays in one spot for a change. This rarely happens! I gladly take advantage of my free time. I can now relax and enjoy myself for a while.

I run up and down the creek bank, barking at the salmon as they skitter back and forth in the shallow water. It is fun to make them scatter in front of me. I feel like a big and powerful queen commanding all of my subjects.

Suddenly, without warning, the wind brings me a scent I have never smelled before. I run back to my person, folding up and stretching out in long arching leaps, in urgent haste to warn her of coming danger. She scoops me up in her arms and whispers, "grizzly bear" in my ear. From my higher vantage point, I can now see him. I understand from her tenseness that this animal is different. As it comes lumbering up the creek, its smell becomes stronger and pungent to me. I decide I had better be silent and motionless this time. I could not bark anyway, as my person clutches me so tightly while holding that box up to her face, that she squeezes the breath out of me. I hear her whisper; "I never miss a good photographic opportunity" and the black box blinks to life.

As the huge, shaggy, dripping wet bear approaches, I hear the clicking sound of the box, the distant shrill cry of a bald eagle, and the water splashing from the bear's movement. The bear walks so close I can see the whites of his eyes when he cocks them to watch us as he shuffles by, his ears twitching with each click of the box. I try to curl my toes away from him. Right about now I am wishing the bank was higher above the creek. My

Annie and the Grizzly

Miniature Dachshund size feels insufficient. If only I was as big as that bear, I would make sure he does not bother my person. I estimate only a few Dachshund lengths between him and my toes as he saunters by below us. The salmon scatter and skitter away in great splashing waves to keep from becoming a lunch snack for the bear. I hear a few more clicks from the box at my person's eyes. Ambling on past us, the bear displays no interest in exchanging sniffing. He only continues cautiously watching us. The hair on the back of my neck stands on end, the only thing about me that moves. I feel unnerved, unsettled, perturbed, and psyched out. Even my person holds her breath.

I certainly have no interest in meeting and sniffing with the Grizzly. I may be mouthy and pushy at times, but I also know when to be prudent. After he rounds the bend and heads upstream toward the glacier, I look at my person, she looks at me, and we breathe a collective sigh of relief. Tomorrow, new predicaments and adventure await us. I intend to use my good nose, sharp bark, and alert vigilance to keep us safe just as I always do.

Page 21

Jan Greenlee Abbott

Jan was born in Spokane, Washington and lived in Seattle for many years. In high school, she was published by and received a scholarship from *Guideposts* magazine. As a prize for an essay, she spent a summer in Athens, Greece. She holds a B.A. in English. For 15 years, she worked in computer operations, network administration, and PC support, documenting extensively. She is currently devoting her time to creative writing. Two cats allow Jan and her husband to live with them in Poquoson, Virginia. Jan has known and loved many animals over the years, including Babe (of French fry fame), Libby, & Tai.

Libby Greenlee Abbott is a 17-year-old female calico whose voice narrates "The Feline Mystique." She deigns to live with Jan.

Tai Greenlee Abbott was one of three Samoyeds adopted over the years by Jan's family in Spokane. They thoroughly enjoyed each other's company for 10 years. His experiences inspired "A Dog's Day."

The Feline Mystique
(A Guide for the Young Female)
by Libby as told to Jan Greenlee Abbott

As you prepare to leave the litter, I want to review some lessons we've been covering. I've tried to keep them in order of importance. You know them well by now, but indulge your mother. These rules have been passed down from generation to generation, my girl, and you can never underestimate their value. You may be swayed by vague affection for the humans sometimes, but never let that deter you. They were put on earth for our use and pleasure, and not the other way around. After all, you are the rightful Ruler of the Universe and Mistress of All You

Survey. This reality lays the groundwork for all these guidelines.

Naming: People call us cat. Actually, they call you many names in many tones of voice, some of them quite derogatory. For example, I have been called Bane of Their Existence, although I prefer Queen of All I Survey, Dominatrix of the Universe, and Empress of the Known World (or all that is worth knowing).

Whatever and whenever they call you, either ignore them or take a considerable amount of time when responding, unless it is feeding time. Then you can be quite demonstrative. Always remember you are the owner, not the mortal.

Sleeping: Anytime is a good time to nap. After all, training the food sources, maintaining our dignity, eating upon demand, and lounging about are all very strenuous activities.

Anywhere is a good place to sleep, the higher and warmer the better. I have found that the top of a recording VCR is a good place for an afternoon nap. I also like heat registers. If the bipeds or other objects get in your way, go over them. (See also **Boundaries.)** Couches, beds, drawers, and stairs are all good places to sleep. One cat I know likes to sleep in laundry baskets, preferably full of warm, clean clothes. Another cat has efficiently combined our two favorite activities by sleeping in his food dish. Feel free to be creative.

If you sleep with people, don't worry about disturbing them (as if any self-respecting cat would). Follow your routine, no matter what the time. If your place happens to be on their face, arms, legs, stomach, back, or any other body part, so be it. (See also **Gravity**.) Now, sleeping with or on these creatures may give them the impression you like them. We know this isn't necessarily the case, but allow them their illusions. Use them for their body heat.

Wherever you sleep or lounge, remember to bathe thoroughly. Also, make sure that you prepare your spot carefully with much kneading. Never mind if the human disagrees with your choice or timing. Sometimes they get cranky when we make biscuits on their legs or belongings. Ignore them. You know what you prefer, and what you prefer is always right.

Feeding: One of the first rules we covered was this: When you encounter something new, ask yourself, "Can I eat it or will it eat me?" If you can eat it, do so. As domestic cats, we prefer the best but sometimes must make do with what people give us. This usually means canned or dried food. (See also **Toys**.) Since you run the household, be finicky. Make the food sources change your diet by refusing to eat. Force them to progress from the least to the most expensive food - we deserve it.

To get snacks, cry for food even when it's not mealtime. Act as if you haven't been fed for days. Lick anything on the kitchen floor - you never know what you could find, and sometimes the humans feel guilty and feed. Also, they can be forgetful and uncommunicative. Use these facts to get extra helpings.

Of course, people food is much better than cat food. Here are some ways to acquire it. Whenever bipeds eat, get underfoot. If they aren't too spiteful, linger by the table at mealtimes, looking as pitiful as possible. If you're alert, you can grab morsels falling from the table. (You can also try snatching food from the table or counters, but the consequences are usually unpleasant.) Remember, these activities should not be confused with begging. I have caught you begging like a dog, for which you were severely disciplined. I brought you up better than that.

The Feline Mystique

Individuals that we are, cats each have their own food preferences. Whatever you eat, always remember to bury the food after you're finished, even if you're indoors. Eating regularly, which means whenever you want, is crucial to maintaining your strength and therefore your dominance. Unfortunately, the mortals feed us when they want. This conflict is easily resolved. If they don't feed you when you want in the morning (usually at dawn), yowl at the top of your lungs. Siamese cats are especially gifted, but all of us have some talent. Work those vocal cords!* If the humans continue to ignore you, jump on various body parts. This tends to get their attention. If they have the effrontery to strike you, hiss and strike back before strategically withdrawing. Some cats have found that rapidly walking across the pillows is effective. Others pat the person's face, often but not always with claws retracted. Use your own judgment and do whatever works.

Once feeding times are established to your satisfaction, never let them vary. If meals are late, complain incessantly until you're fed. After all, we have other things to do. (See **Sleeping**.) The same holds true if people try to change mealtimes. Follow the morning wakeup routine at any time of day or night until your schedule is reestablished. This takes about a week. Remember, you must <u>never</u> let mortals think they are dominant. They are our minions; treat them accordingly.

Toys: When encountering something new, a corollary to "Can I eat it?" is "Can I play with it?" Dry food doubles as both food and toy, as does wild prey. If you are inside, many objects will do, including people. Whether you attack their toes, fingers, or legs, they can jump and scream quite satisfactorily - always good for a smile. You

---

* People talk to us; initiate the conversation. Practice screaming at 2 or 3 in the morning just for fun.

may enjoy the cheesy toys they get for us, but be discerning. Above all, do not play on demand except if it strikes your fancy. To do otherwise demeans your dignity and could give the mortals the erroneous impression they are in control.

Dignity: Dignity must be preserved at any cost. If your dignity should be compromised (e.g, catnip), act offended and stalk away. (If you're unsure whether your dignity has been compromised, being laughed at is a good clue.) After you deign to return, be sure and punish the offenders thoroughly by giving them withering looks and ignoring any friendly overtures. If done well, this also can result in more food.

Bathing: When in doubt, bathe. Looking good is key to getting food and attention. Any time (even during a cat altercation) and any place is a good time for a bath.

Gravity: Since we are the center of the universe, it is only logical we are one with the center of the earth. This truism is especially handy in wintertime. As long as you remember this, you cannot be easily dislodged from where you want to be.

Vets, Medicine, Baths, Children, and Other Nuisances: The general rule of paw when suffering these tortures: Cling to any available surface (human or material) and be as disagreeable and vocal as possible. Remember, claws and teeth are your friends. Properly punish everyone and everything involved afterwards.

Affection: While it is rumored we have some affection for our people, this never has been nor will be documented. While it may or may not be true, they must never get the sustained impression we care for them.

Boundaries: All boundaries are arbitrary and inherently meaningless. After all, you are a superior being and should be able to go anywhere any time you want. Enforce this lesson by hesitating when bipeds open the door for you. Go in and out as often as possible. Keep life interesting by rushing through doors when they least expect it.

Allow nothing to get in your way, including mortals. Ignore their protestations (as if they really mattered). Jump on any furniture or high surface in the place, including refrigerators. After all, you are the Queen of All You Survey, and there's more to survey from high places.

As I've said, these are just the basics. There are other rules and rituals I've neglected to mention, but a feline must have some secrets. We must put up with people, at least until we develop opposable thumbs. Besides, they are excellent sources of heat, food, toys, and affection. Forgive them their failings - they're <u>only</u> human.

The Cat Who Loved French Fries
by Jan Greenlee Abbott

I once lived with a cat named Babe, who indeed loved French fries. In fact, he loved food of any sort and went to great lengths to procure it. Babe also loved looking good, being loved, and loving me, possibly not in that order. His was not a quiet love.

First to the fries. They had to be freshly killed by being thrown up in the air and pounced on a couple of times before Babe would eat them. He also loved hamburger, steak, and bacon. These did not have to be killed; they could be eaten directly. Babe wasn't confined to plebeian tastes. As a young cat, he was fond of champagne, and he loved lobster throughout his life. When he was older, Babe developed feline uterine syndrome and was on prescription dry food. He would fish each piece out of the bowl, bat it across the kitchen floor, bounce it off the refrigerator, and finally eat it. While this sounds cute, it lost its charm when we lived in a one-bedroom apartment and he ate late at night. I would hear shuffle, shuffle, bat, bat, bat, blam, bat, blam, crunch, crunch. By the tenth or twentieth repetition, I would yell, "Damn it, Babe, be bold and eat a whole mouthful."

Babe's oral fetish was apparent early in his life. When he was a kitten, he suckled my tee shirt. I feared I would go through life with an ever-increasing Babe hanging from my shirt. Fortunately for us both, he gave up suckling before then.

I didn't know when Babe crossed the line from healthy to portly. You see, he was half Persian, half Siamese, all white with red points, so he always looked plump. I thought he was a chubby kitten until I gave him a bath and found there wasn't much cat under all that fur. Of course, more meals followed until he reached his prime weight of 14 pounds.

Babe's quest for food emboldened him. One day I left meat defrosting on the kitchen counter. Hearing strange sounds emanating from the kitchen, I found Babe dragging a steak across the floor.

Babe didn't limit himself to counters or kitchens. The night before he was neutered, he obviously had no supper. I awoke to an odd sound at 3:00 a.m. I saw Babe perched precariously on top of the bedroom door with a confused look on his face, a feat he could accomplish only by leaping on a chair and then 3-5 feet up to the doorjamb. Since I didn't want him to fall, I said conversationally, "Babe, how the hell did you get up there?" He looked at me as if to say, "I really don't know, Mom, but there's no food up here," and then leaped back down.

Babe showed his athleticism and creativity when I tried to bathe him. He panicked from beginning to end. He is the only cat I've ever seen who tried to crawl up the inside of a faucet.

Babe was not always a graceful or wise athlete. In one apartment, I watched him investigate an empty box, then later leap on its flap, falling completely into the box. In the same apartment, the kitchen window faced my neighbor's living room. While visiting her, I would see my other cat poised elegantly in my windowsill. Then I would watch Babe leap to the window, bounce off the glass, and miss the sill. His front paws futilely tried to cling to the glass until his desperate face disappeared from sight.

Perhaps his vision wasn't good; Babe consistently miscalculated leaps to the couch and chairs, slithering off either. He didn't corner well. When he chased my other cat, I often heard him crash into walls. I learned the sounds a cat makes when he jumps on the washer, slides across it, plunges behind it, and frantically tries to get out.

Another morning, well after Babe's dawn wake-the dead-feed-me-Siamese yowl, I fell back asleep and woke to yet another odd noise. I saw Babe hanging from the curtain attached by his claws. Often I would hear a rustling sound and find Babe slouching to another room dragging a full-size afghan behind him. He never got the hang of retraction.

Babe wasn't the only one to miscalculate. When he was a kitten, I would reach out my foot to rub his belly, and he would attack my foot. I thought it was cute. Occasionally, when he was grown, I would do the same and find myself perched on one foot with a 14-pound cat, claws and all, nailed to my other leg and foot.

The Cat Who Loved French Fries

Babe continued his love affair with feet. He slept with his face in shoes. He was particularly fond of toes. One morning, I awoke to a pinprick sensation in my big toe, which was sticking out from under the covers. When I moved, the cat went into full attack mode on my foot. Thereafter, I didn't move when Babe inserted one claw into my exposed toe.

Other times, Babe used his paws for benign purposes. Once I threw myself on the bed sobbing over some heartbreak. I felt a gentle tapping on my arm. It was Babe, patting me on the arm as if to say, "It's all right, Mom, I'm here." Another morning, I awoke to a gentle tap, tap on my face and found Babe looking at me. When I realized I'd overslept, he got many "good cats" (and probably more breakfast). When he slept with me, he kept one paw on my arm.

Babe was a love cat. When I first saw him at the pet store, he was chasing his littermates. I reached out, scratched him under the chin, and he fell over purring. His legs kept moving, but apparently petting was too wonderful to bypass. Babe had a loud motor and was easily induced to purr. When we later lived in a two-story house, I would pet Babe, go upstairs to bed, and still hear him purring contentedly downstairs.

Although loving, Babe knew that looking good was key to his survival. I found him staring in a vanity mirror one day. Naively, I thought he wanted to play with the strange cat. Then he looked in the mirror, licked down a stray piece of fur, inspected himself again, and kept on grooming until he looked perfect. Vanity, thy name was Babe.

He was usually (and oddly) obedient for a cat. He would come when I snapped my fingers. Of course, I usually fed or petted him. However, he was disobedient when hunting.

Pawprints on My Heart

Babe didn't confine himself to domestic prey. As much as a cowardly lion as he was (a friend once remarked she was amazed that so big a cat could slink so low to the ground), I was surprised when Babe turned out to be a hunter late in life. He kept my spider population down. One night, as I was eating dinner in the den, I noticed Babe playing with something. He was tossing a vole up in the air and catching it on the way down. When the rodent landed on the recliner, I decided that was enough and disposed of it. Staring at me with crossed blue eyes, Babe was quite upset.

Another day, Babe met me when I came home and followed me upstairs, as usual. When I was changing in the walk-in closet, I heard brushing against the wall. Thinking it must be a big moth, I looked up to see a small brown bird. The bird flew out the door. Babe pursued. As I was frantically throwing on clothes, I heard a thud in the hallway. Somewhat dressed, I dashed out. Babe was on the stairs with the bird in his mouth. I chased him down the stairs, through the living and dining rooms, and back up the stairs, but Babe never relinquished the bird. (I guess he had learned from the vole incident.) He always had intestinal problems, but apparently bird agreed with him. Later, all I found was one large feather and four pinfeathers.

Babe is gone now. My spider population is up. Fortunately, no other wild creatures have made it into the house, as my current cats, although equally cherished, aren't quite the hunter Babe was. I harbor hopes for the "new" cat evolving into a hunter. (Last week, he stalked a tree as I dragged it across the yard.) Babe's lifetime roommate still deigns to share the house with me.

My life is quieter now. I don't always wake at dawn, but then again, I don't hear Babe's purring last thing at night. I am comforted knowing Babe had lobster his last

The Cat Who Loved French Fries

Christmas (and was positively aggressive about eating it). In his last days, he perked up when he saw a wild bird loose in a clinic. Babe's last meal was hash browns from MacDonald's. (It was too early for French fries.) Now, whenever I see those little brown birds, I think of them as "Babe Bites".

A Dog's Day
by Jan Greenlee Abbott

"You're getting on my last nerve, dog," the man warned as he drove me to the vet.

What had I done?

"First, you keep me up half the night barking at coyotes."

I was only protecting you, I thought.

"Then there was the bath, and the cows, and now this. You're just a no-good, coyote barking, cat cringing, cow chasing, porcupine eating, worthless excuse for a dog. I've a mind to leave you at the vet!" he blustered.

A Dog's Day

My terrible dog day was about to get worse.

It had all started with the screen door opening. "Get out if you're going out, cats," the man growled. The cats grudgingly obliged, then sniffed my nose. I looked at the man hopefully, but he just murmured, "Later, boy."

The cats recoiled from the damp and retreated back to the covered porch. I could have told them it was raining, but the cats rarely listen to me. I hoped we could share the porch, but the female disagreed. After she smacked me across the nose, I lay in my usual spot under a pine tree.

The screen door slammed.

The man came out grumbling, "Don't know why she can't do her own shopping." Dodging the cats, he said, "No, you aren't going back inside. Where's that dog?" He looked around and saw me. "Dog, you're letting those cats lead you around by the nose again," he said disgustedly. I got up, tail wagging, sock in mouth. "No, I can't play with you. I've got to go shopping," he sneered. My long, white tail drooped as he roared away in the truck.

When it stopped raining, the cats decided to go hunting. I didn't want to go, but the female insisted with another nose smacking. I trotted off into the field with the two cats.

Catching the scintillating scent of mole, I followed it to the mound. Dirt flew from all directions as the rodent burrowed deeper. How I love a good dig! That mole was no match for me. I didn't care when the cats chased me away to make the kill. The thrill was in the hunt.

On the way back through the pasture, I treated myself to a hearty roll. Who could resist the seductive scent of cow dung? I went home a happy, albeit now green, dog.

I bounded up to the man, but he was less than pleased to see me.

Drawing back, he said, "What have you gotten yourself into, dog? Don't answer; I know. Phew!" He disappeared into the shed to return with the dreaded washtub.

Oh, no, I thought, not the bath. I crouched down and thought about escape.

"No, you don't," the man responded, filling the tub. "You're not getting out of this. As if I don't have enough to do, now I have to give you a bath!" he groused. "Come on, get in the tub."

It was the only way to please him. I got in the warm, soapy water reluctantly. Afterwards, I shook off the foul stuff as best I could.

"Don't...don't!" the man spluttered, but it was too late. He was already drenched. "Great. Now I've got to change clothes. In the shop you go."

I wandered disconsolately around the shop, my long, currently pitiful tail drooping. I just couldn't do anything right today. What could I do to make amends?

Finally, the man let me out, and I followed him to the pasture. He said to no one in particular, "See that steer? He's fattening up nicely. I don't like the looks of that heifer, though it's hard to tell from this far away."

That was it! Although I hadn't had much practice, Samoyeds are herding dogs by trade. I could herd the cows toward him so he could get a better view. I crawled under the fence, losing a little of my long, white hair in the barbed wire. It was a small price to pay to make the man happy. I snuck up on the cows, and then I charged, curved tail arched proudly above my back. The herd stampeded away from me. As we neared the man, I could hear him shouting, but his words were lost in the din. I glanced at him and was confounded by his beet-red face.

"What on God's green earth do you think you're doing?" he shouted.

A Dog's Day

At that moment, one of the cows stopped and turned to confront me. I decided the better part of wisdom was retreat. I tucked my tail between my legs and ran, emitting high-pitched "EE-EE-EE" sounds as I went.

I heard the man yelling amidst laughter, "I guess that's a case of the dumb chasing the dumber."

That hurt. I can take a lot, but that was too much, even from the man. I slunk into the woods and then took a long walk to salve my pride. I caught wind of an unfamiliar scent and followed it down to the orchard. The stronger it was, the more enticing. I simply had to know this creature. A vague foreboding shadowed my zeal, but I brushed it aside. A dog has to do what a dog has to do, and this odor was simply irresistible. At last, I found the source trapped by an apple tree. I nosed in, just to say hi. The porcupine moved back, uttering unprintable phrases about me and the man. Vague dread increasing, I warned it; it continued its barrage of insults. I snapped at it, but it kept maligning us. It had to be silenced. I shook some sense into it. SPROING! My reward was a mouthful of quills. To put it mildly, YIPES! YEOW! OUCH!

That and many dog epithets ran through my mind as I hightailed it (figuratively if not literally) back home. Scrambling onto the porch, I gulped water frantically. The more I lapped, the worse the needles pricked. Desperately, I tried to brush them away with my paws, but the stinging only got worse. I was one doleful dog.

The man came up to the porch. "Sorry about that cow remark, boy. Sorry about a lot of things," he sighed, squatting beside me. "Just because I'm in a foul mood, I shouldn't take it out on you." He paused. "Boy? What's wrong with you, boy?" He saw the quills in my nose. "Damn it, dog, not again," he muttered as he got the leash.

In the car, the man vented. "You're just a no-good, coyote-barking, cat-cringing, cow-chasing, porcupine-eating, worthless excuse for a dog. I've a mind to leave you at the vet!"

I was in a world of hurt.

He continued, "I've had it with you. I mean it this time!"

Could he really mean it?

"Yeah, I really, really mean it this time!"

Dejected, I slumped down in the seat. When we stopped at the vet's, I rubbed up against the man, but he shoved me toward the door. Big, liquid brown eyes begging for a reprieve, I planted all four feet as firmly as I could on the sidewalk, but eventually the man dragged in all 80 pounds of me.

When I saw the vet, he poked, prodded, and pulled. The prickling in my mouth and nose subsided, but I felt no better. The vet disappeared. His assistant gave me some water and tried to comfort me, but what I really wanted was the man. Where was he? Had he indeed left me? I lay on the floor, tender nose between my paws. Maybe he was right. Maybe I was a no-good dog who deserved to be abandoned.

"Pretty horrible day, wasn't it, boy?" The man knelt beside me, attaching the leash.

He hadn't left me! I nudged him gently.

"There's enough time for that when we get home," he said, getting up. Amazed, I trotted to the car.

On the way home, the man muttered, "What does that vet know, anyway? Okay, maybe your kind does chase reindeer for a living, but I don't think reindeer look like cows."

My instincts say they do, I thought. Tentatively, I licked his hand.

"Gotta drive, boy," he brushed me away. He sighed. "Maybe it's true that no dog can stop chasing porcupines."

Other dogs did this? I thought, relieved.

A Dog's Day

"But did you really have to get in the manure?" he continued.

How could I resist?

"I guess you can't help being a dog."

No, I really couldn't. My tail started wagging.

"You are a pretty good watchdog."

I'll be right here to make sure you're protected, I thought. My tail wagged harder.

"I'm not giving in on the cats, though. Listen to me. No dog of mine lets cats chase him off his own porch."

He had a point. I licked his face.

"Quit mushing on me," he said gruffly, but he smiled as he rubbed my ears. "Let's keep this between us, okay?"

Who was I going to tell?

The rest of the drive was filled with companionable silence.

When we got home, cats went flying as I charged to my rightful place on the porch.

"Way to go, boy!" The man said softly as he went indoors.

Later that night the coyotes started howling. I barked fiercely, proving what a good watchdog I was. I told those coyotes in no uncertain terms that this was my territory and these were my people and they best stay away if they didn't want trouble.

As the man opened the door, I heard him mutter something to the woman about shutting up that no-good, coyote barking dog. When the door closed, we both hesitated.

When he was sure we were alone, he reached down and patted me roughly, saying, "That's a good dog." As he sat and loved me, I dozed off to catless, bathless, porcupineless, vetless dreams of frolicking in a fresh foot of snow with my owner.

Page 41

Phyllis Harwood

A lifetime resident of Gloucester, Virginia, Phyllis Harwood's experiences include work as a trained x-ray technician and with the local newspaper. Married with two children, she has now semi-retired and enjoys volunteer work, gardening, and writing poetry. Her lifelong love of dogs started as a child, with a collie-mix named Lady. Over the next 30 years, a parade of long-haired dachshunds continued to claim Phyllis as their special human companion. Most recently she offered her home and love to a rescued Papillon named Miss BeBe. Today, two young Papillons, three mix-breed rescues and two cats occupy her time but do not keep her from writing both poetry and prose.

Requiem for a Rescue
by Phyllis Harwood

I didn't start out to adopt an old dog. Certainly, I didn't plan to give my heart to a twelve-year old. Some of life's finest gifts just seem to happen in spite of our planning, however. And so it was when I adopted an elderly Papillon named Miss BeBe just short of her thirteenth birthday. Through our three years together I learned a great deal about Papillons: their assertiveness and courage, the needs and habits of an elderly dog, and the steadfast love that is a part of every canine but especially obvious with this little rescue. Most of all she taught me the meaning of holding fast to a dream.

Requiem for a Rescue

Our story, BeBe's and mine, began as stories often do, with sad loses in both our lives. Her mistress got a new job, a new apartment, and didn't want BeBe any more. I lost my dearest fuzzy face Doc, the last in a long line of dachshunds.

I'd shared my life with long-haired dachshunds for almost 30 straight years. After Doc's death, I just needed to grieve. My resolve to go without another companion lasted about a month. Then I decided to get a repair kit for the big hole in my heart. I expanded my search for a new companion to include a Papillon, since I had seen a papillon puppy at a dog show. The tiny face with big ears intrigued me, as did the descriptions of the breed I'd unearthed in my reading. I planned to search for a dachshund puppy, or a papillon puppy or a shelter dog, and start a new relationship with whichever one I located first that seemed to click with me.

I started checking newspaper ads, found a few for doxies, but none for paps. Undeterred, I pursued my quest with calls to vets, and the local kennel club secretary. My persistence was finally rewarded by contact with a Papillon breeder who invited me over for a visit to meet her pack. There was even a young male that was available for adoption.

I was so excited. Meeting a large group of papillons in their own home was a delight. They ranged in age from 10 months to 14 years, and I was especially taken with one 12-year-old female named Fallon. She seemed to be the official hostess of the house. I would swear, if I did such, that Fallon gently climbed on the sofa beside me to inquire if I'd like one lump of sugar or two in my tea. The breeder smiled at my infatuation with the elderly canine hostess, saying that all visitors fell in love with that particular champion. I was distressed to discover that I did not seem to click with Fallon's great-grandson, however, the young male that was looking for a home. He wasn't a puppy and was far more independent than I wanted.

I returned home to think, or more accurately, to brood about the whole matter. I talked to myself, my daughter, my vet and anyone else with ears. I was so unhappy. With the wisdom and straight thinking of youth, my daughter finally advised me, "If you don't click, you don't click. There are other dogs, so call the breeder back and tell her you aren't interested in the young male." So I did. I was grateful that I got a recording. I didn't have to talk to the breeder and just left a message. I was certain the breeder would be upset about a lost sale and I'd never hear from her again. How wrong I was! In a few days, the breeder called to say she understood and agreed with my assessment that the young male was not right for me. But, she asked, would I consider giving an elderly rescue a home.

She explained that she knew little about the rescue, who she said was called Miss BeBe, except that she was in good health for a dog nearing thirteen. The vet who had attended her since puppyhood had refused to euthanize her when requested to do so. At the vet's request, the owner agreed to sign over the old dog and let the vet find her a new home. The vet had placed Miss BeBe in one home, which didn't work out well because of a young child. Next, he'd tried to locate a Papillon rescue group. One of his patients put him in touch with the breeder I'd visited in Williamsburg, and she offered to give Miss BeBe a home for the remainder of her life.

When my husband found out how old Miss BeBe was he asked if I wanted him to go ahead and dig a hole for her in our pet cemetery out back of our home. He figured she wouldn't last long. But I had read that Papillons often live to 16 years of age, and my heart ached for this little oldie even though I'd never met her. I thought about it for a full twenty-four hours before calling back to say I'd like to meet Miss BeBe. And on July 5, 1996 I went back to Williamsburg to meet her in person.

I cried when I saw her drooling, sad face. As I held this soft, bony, forlorn little lady dog in my arms, I knew it was a pairing meant to be. I promised her that only death would part us from each other--no more strange people, although I'm sure she thought us strange, and no other strange new homes.

In the months and years that followed, BeBe allowed me into her life, but only on the edge, never near the preciously guarded center. That center belonged to the one she loved best, the one for whom she always waited and looked for to the end of her days.

I had her about five months before she showed any interest in me. She tolerated my care and affection, but would then sashay off to another room. I kept the phone line busy talking to the breeder who'd placed BeBe in my care. 'What was I doing wrong? What else could I do?" From BeBe there were no kisses, no cuddles, no affection, just tolerance, and not well hidden at that!

By now, the mutual concern for this unhappy little waif had drawn the breeder and me together and cemented a warm and lasting friendship. She had become simply my friend Jean. We spent long hours sharing many things including Papillons. We struggled to try to refocus our way of thinking to view the world through this little lady dog's eyes. I was coming to realize that to BeBe, the vet had simply misplaced her, failing to return her to the owner she loved as he had done all the previous times in her life. And so she tolerated me as her caregiver while waiting, hoping that every hour and visitor to our door would be her beloved mistress, coming to take her to her old home.

In desperation, Jean sent over a young puppy, Princess, as a friend for Miss BeBe, and as competition for food and affection. The new arrival stimulated a little more interest in food, but little jealousy for attention.

Pawprints on My Heart

A bit of thaw occurred, however, just before Princess arrived. BeBe scratched me on the ankle with her paw, her first sign in five months that she knew I existed. It was a brief but welcomed sign. I loved her head, and she went off into the other room.

I fixed baskets, blankets, and coats for BeBe, my little old lady, to keep her comfortable and warm and because it just seemed like the thing to do for such a dignified lady. She thought little of the coats, but seemed to realize that they kept her warm, so she put up with them. After Princess came to join our group, the coats were a convenient handle by which Princess attempted to pull BeBe around or entice her to play.

BeBe slept with me almost from the day she came into my home. Sometimes, accidentally I'm sure, she snuggled close, but more often she stayed as far away as it was possible to get in a twin size bed. She let me know her needs. I often got long stares from her when it was time for her to go to bed and I was reading. After a few stares, however, she would give up and go to lie in one of her conveniently placed fancy pink baskets to wait for me to take her into the bedroom and on to the bed.

Val, another of Jean's children, joined us in May of 1997. Val and Princess were the constant shadows and attention-demanding companions for which the breed is famous. Now my progress around the house featured a parade of three papillons, but BeBe always brought up the rear and was never really interested in any of us.

Despite the temporary nature in which BeBe regarded her living arrangements, she nonetheless established her feeding requirements very early in our association. "Commercial dog food is for dogs" was her motto, and she obviously did not consider herself a dog! She loved meat sauce served with mashed spaghetti. Her second choice was raw or cooked finely chopped beef. Other acceptable food offerings were macaroni and cheese (mashed if you please), finely broken McDonald's cheeseburgers (hold the pickle and the bread please), and finely chopped chicken or turkey.

She preferred to sleep late--and undisturbed! On days when I volunteered or needed to go out before 10 am, she was offered food at 6 am which she rarely ate. Her other three daily feedings, at 2 pm, 6 pm and again at 11 pm, were treated with patience, restraint, or just ignored, depending on the whims of the moment and her ranking of importance of the food offering. After Princess and Val came to live with us, BeBe's dishes had to be carefully protected from the gluttonous interest of the two younger paps. But she didn't seem to care whether the two stole her food or not.

For the first few months after BeBe came to live with me, she'd go and come between the house and fenced-in yard by herself, returning from outside to frisk around with her butt in the air, and her front paws stretched out in front as if inviting someone to play. Sometimes she even held her tail up a little, but not for long, and she never curled it over her back.

As the months turned into years, age took it toll. For the last six months or so of her life, her mainstay was baby food, veal and turkey being her favorites. Any tasty treat I could offer, I did, but they were rarely acceptable. I carried her up and down the steps between the house and her small yard for many months before her death. In March of 1999, she went in for her annual immunization and check-up. I was told that her lungs sounded like a many-year, many-pack-a-day smoker. My vet said little more, except the vague instruction to take her home and love her -- which I did, had been doing and would always do. If my friend Jean read anything more into my vet's cryptic message, she did not say. She often brought her aging sixteen-year-old Mischief over to visit. We would gossip while Princess and Val jumped around and played, begging to be scratched, petted, noticed. Mischief would sit quietly, on or touching Jean at all times and grumbling whenever the two young Paps came near his mistress. BeBe checked the incoming visitors to see if her long lost owner had come and retreated to one of her baskets and ignored us thereafter.

BeBe waited patiently and quietly through all our months and years together for the old mistress who never came. She whined, a low hoarse noise, only a few times in her life with me, and that when she slipped down the blanket to the floor at the foot of the bed. Mostly BeBe was silent, very silent, waiting and listening.

Then two days before her death, she had two seizures, one each day. She made a rapid, hoarse bark at the beginning of each seizure. I was not overly fearful. Jean's Mischief had been on preventative for seizures for the previous eight months, so I took BeBe to my vet expecting to be given medication to control her seizures.

Instead, my vet gave me the distressing news that BeBe had only a few days at most to live, that she was drowning in her own fluid. Through tears, I chose to let her go as peacefully as possible since there was no hope of recovery, no future except to struggle for breath.

I miss BeBe. She was a stately, little lady dog. I always hoped for a breakthrough in our relationship, but our best effort was just friends. BeBe was ever true to her original human. I always hoped somehow she would see her human again. Maybe she will.......over the Rainbow Bridge.

To BeBe, my little rescue who lived with me and my family for almost 3 years. She was ever loyal to her original owner of approximately 12 years. I truly hope BeBe's human will meet her at the Rainbow Bridge.

Miss BeBe's Refrain
August 11, 1983 - May 22, 1999
By Phyllis Harwood

I am confused, so sad, forlorn.
As first I met you on that morn.
With tearfilled eyes, you softly said,
"We'll be together, till one is dead."
So it began, our journey strange.
You did your best to ease my pain.
As months and then the years went by
You seemed to know my silent cry.
You're just not HER. Oh, can't you see,
I know she's coming back for me.
She's coming back and I must go.
She is my human, don't you know.
She'll pick me up with eyes aglow,
And scratch behind my ears just so.
And tell me lovingly and great
Just how she kept my dish and plate
For my return to her dear care.
She's coming back, my love to share.
But I'll abide with you awhile,
Just don't expect my eyes to smile.
No happy tail or loving rub
Or playful time in the bubble tub.
I guess I'll let you love my head,
Because I do enjoy your bed.

Pawprints on My Heart

I even snuggle when it's cold.
I guess it's 'cause I'm getting old.
Those coats you make are hard to take,
But my hair is thin and I do quake.
The food is pretty good as well.
With these three teeth I can't quite tell!
She's coming back and I must go.
I can't relax. I miss HER so.
I search in every room and place,
And yet I can not find a trace.
My eyes are dim, my hearing's bad.
She holds my heart and I'm so sad.
Oh, please come quickly, so I can go
To be with you in a place I know.
The vet says it is time to go.
I feel so bad; my breathing's slow.
But wait....I must press on you see
I know she's coming back for me.
The end has come and YOU'RE with me.
Oh, where, oh, where, can my lady be?
Your eyes are wet, your voice is soft.
"I love you, BeBe," as I drift off.
The Rainbow Bridge is where I'll be.
I know she's coming there for me.

Two Blessings

by Phyllis Harwood

When last I wrote, I was so sad.
    Miss Be was gone and that was bad.
But the story doesn't stop, you see--
    Miss Be was one of a royal three.
Miss Be--a rescue, quite old to boot.
    A disposable love who was quite cute.
These two were part of a treasured pack
    And young and frisky and quite an act.
And though they came to help Miss Be,
    They leapt into my heart with glee.
End tables weren't the safest place
    To leave one's nail boards or sewing lace.
Mystery bad guys and cats to chase.
    The other dogs to keep in place.
A never ending job, you see
    For the two small dogs who came to me.
"Full body rubs" were their request
    And "Are you asleep?" as they stand on my chest.
Adoring eyes and sweetest kisses
    A host and hostess for their missus".
Val and Prin, I do salute
    Life with you is quite a hoot!
Our lives do change--but on we go
    To see the future friend or foe.
I'm not alone on sunset street
    I have two blessings at my feet.

Val's Poem

I hid my bone in a potato bin,
     Doo dah doo dah,
Prin found it and is chewing it again,
     Oh, dah doo dah day.

Princess' Poem

I'm chewing Val's bone and making him whine,
     Doo dah, doo dah,
He hides it in the same place every time,
     Oh, dah doo dah day.

John Atkinson

Born in Richmond, Virginia many moons ago, John Atkinson now resides on Gwynns' Island, Virginia with his wife, Reneé, and Jody, a Sheltie dog. One of eight children, John has three married daughters and four grandchildren. His days are devoted to writing and gardening. John won first place in adult fiction at the 1998 Chesapeake Writer's Conference. Many of his short stories have been published in magazines and newspapers. His first book, a novella entitled *Mercy Me,* was published in May, 2000.

The Trip

by John Atkinson

The three hundred horsepower V8 rumbled the instant I turned the key. My Sheltie dog, Jody, was at my side. Reneé, my wife, was standing at the window.

"Do you know how ridiculous you look?" she asked, holding her hips.

I knew. But after thirty years of marriage, I also knew when she was toying with me.

"Our neighbors must think you're crazy - you take that old car in and out of the garage two and three times a day."

The Trip

I didn't care if they did. I remained silent. Jody liked the hundred foot trip from the carriage house to the giant maple tree in our front yard. On our trip I'd talked about old times.

"Stop acting foolish!" Reneé snapped.

I winked at her, closed the door to the big sedan and gently backed out into the sunlight.

I said, "Jody, when I was young, I wanted a car like this. Man, could I do some traveling!"

I heard Reneé yelling, but Jody and I hit the accelerator and drove away slowly like always. We could see her in the rear mirror waving with one hand and smiling.

"Little fellow, women don't know much about traveling fever," I said seriously. "You know, now that all the children are grown, I'm at liberty to let my mind drift back to my youth - to my traveling days. It's good to dream on these little trips." Jody seemed to understand my sentiments. "Can you feel the power of this baby? Man, look at that hood. You want to drive? Here, get behind the wheel." Jody climbed into my lap. "No, don't lick me - keep your eyes on the road."

We soon reached the end of our journey - the old tree. Jody was as happy as if we had driven to the moon.

"Look who's caught up with us," I pointed to Reneé standing by my window again.

"You've got work to do," she said.

"Work can wait. Jody wants to hear about Mesa Verde, Colorado."

Reneé said something, but neither Jody nor I could understand her over the blaring radio.

The inevitable came minutes later. I had completed my story and our little trip. Jody appeared content in my lap. I thought, what if we humans could be satisfied with such a short ride? Maybe in Jody's mind we had visited the Mesa. That was a pleasant thought and I hugged him.

Reneé asked, "Did you have fun?"

I winked at her but didn't answer.

"It's time to get out, fellow," I said to Jody. "We'll take another ride after lunch. Then I'll tell you about Oregon or maybe California."

We got out and Jody's herding instinct kicked in. He circled the old car without license plates and marveled at our ride.

"Keep an eye on her, Jody. She's a jewel in the rough. We'll fix it up some day. Maybe then we can talk grandma into riding back to the barn with us. We can explain that this foolishness of travel is a man thing."

This time Reneé didn't say anything while I continued talking to Jody. "I know, Jody," I rubbed him behind the ear while his eyes were fixed on the sedan, "that's a real traveling machine parked over there, isn't it?"

Little Jody didn't answer me, but his eyes said it all. Like myself, he knows it is.

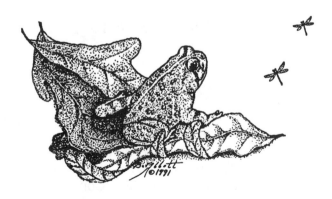

The Bird That Came to Dinner
by John Atkinson

"Boogadee, boogadee, boogadee," I said to our new grandson, Connor Evan. Our youngest child, Lesley, and her husband, Ray, are good parents. Reneé and I visited them a few weeks ago.

"It's time old deeds come home to roost," I said to all within earshot. "I'll tell you one of the many silly things our Lesley did when she was a child, Connor." I explained how one never knows what a child will do next. Although Reneé and I couldn't have asked for a better child, Lesley would astonish us on occasion.

"Boogadee, boogadee, let's go down memory lane," I said, still holding two-month old Connor close to my ribs. "Sometimes you've got to pay your dues, little man." I thought about a brainless dog Lesley had brought home.

"But Dad!" she cried, "it's a Blue Merle Collie."

"Yes, but he doesn't have sense enough to know what "NO" means," I yelled.

After the dog had soiled my clothes with his paws, I watched him run into a tree. "If he's blind," I said, "his nose sure makes up for his lack of sight."

The dog had a nose for home cooking. He would sniff our outside kitchen window whenever you opened the refrigerator. I couldn't eat or grill anything outdoors without having to contend with the dog. Having food on one's person or even old gum wrappers would attract him.

"Little man," I said to Connor, "girls can talk their dads into most anything. Your mom got permission to keep that dog, but only if he didn't wee wee or poopsy or go through a wall in the house. Hey, little man, the dog was dumb, but he had a nose for finding home cooking."

I smiled at Lesley, a first-time mother, and continued teasing. "Boogadee, boogadee, your mom didn't know it, Connor, but after that dumb dog ran through my newly screened door, he had signed his traveling papers."

It was Thanksgiving day about ten years ago and I didn't want to spoil our festivities. Between spells of "composure," I asked Lesley to leash the dog. I guess the smell of Reneé's home cooked food was driving him crazy, because the more Lesley tried to control him, the worse he acted.

Out of breath, Lesley said, "He thinks I'm playing with him, Dad."

"Do you understand that I'm not?" I replied, pointing to the damaged door.

The Bird That Came to Dinner

She finally got the dog restrained. It was an hour before our Thanksgiving meal, which gave me too much time to fret patching the screen.

Still holding my new grandson, I rocked him with "Boogadee, boogadee, boogadee."

While Reneé was waiting patiently for her turn with Connor, I continued telling the tale. "It was after we had said grace when I happened to see your mom's dumb dog coming across our yard with a large object in his mouth. I excused myself from the table and went outside to investigate further. I could hardly believe my eyes, little man. That dumb dog had a whole turkey in his mouth with a thermometer still stuck in its breast. The bird was hot, and according to the pop-up thermometer, it had finished cooking!"

"With a house full, Grandma, Reneé, our three girls and their husbands, it was not a good time to mention the unexpected turkey coming to dinner, but I did. All the girls got upset, but Grandma and Reneé went ballistic because someone, somewhere, was having Thanksgiving dinner ruined by that dumb dog. Also, during all the commotion of phoning everyone we knew to find out whose bird we had was not a good time for me to joke about shooting the dog.

"Yeah, Connor, Grandpa was lucky he got something to eat that day. And the dog with a nose for home cooking got away with ruining our family's meal and someone else's too. We never learned whose bird was stolen."

"Boogadee, boogadee. Reneé it's your turn to hold Connor, but not for too long, because I have a new tale to share. Hurry back, little man. Grandpa can't wait to tell you more tales. Now what kind of doggie would you like to have, grandson? A dumb dog, you say? Well, I think Grandpa can find you one."

Page 61

Joy B. Burch

Joy Brenda Burch lives on the water in Westmoreland County, Virginia near Colonial Beach. She shares her home with Larry Bird, the African Grey and three dogs. She is the guardian of Zach, a Great Dane; Tina, a Miniature Schnauzer; and her "Major Car Dog," a German Shepherd named Engel. She and Engel are inseparable.

Besides her furry and feathered friends, Joy enjoys sailing, sewing, writing, and gardening. She has more time for all these interests since she retired. She is a Registered Nurse and has taught school. She was born in Richmond, Virginia and grew up in Fairfax County. An alumna of The College of William and Mary, she received her nursing diploma from Montreal General Hospital in Quebec, Canada. Joy has enjoyed traveling and working in a variety of settings. She served as a nurse in the U.S. Army during the Vietnam era. After almost 20 years living in Texas (which she loved), Joy returned to the land of her roots, Virginia, twelve years ago. Larry Bird thinks she is a dingleberry.

Good Morning, Larry Bird
by Joy B. Burch

This morning, like all other mornings for the last ten years, I said good morning to Larry Bird. Sometimes he says "Good morning" back to me, but this morning he said, "I love you!" Then he laughed, whistled and walked across his ceiling.

"What?" you say, "Larry Bird could not be in this area…I would have heard something about it."

"What about the play-offs? He is with his team"

Yes, but I am not talking about that Larry Bird. I am talking about Larry Bird, the female African Grey that lives in my house.

Good Morning, Larry Bird

African Greys are parrots that originally came from the Congo area of Africa. They are often referred to as the "Cadillac of talking birds." Not only that, African Greys are said to have the intelligence of a four-year old and the emotional development of a two-year-old child. That makes for a very "brainy brat." My Larry Bird certainly fits that description. Larry delights my day with laughing (he sounds like me), squeaky door noises (I must oil those hinges), the icemaker dumping a tray of fresh ice, knocking on the door, barking, blowing a nose, coughing with a wheeze, sniffing, opening an aluminum can with a pull tab, a pouring beverages sound and various clicking and humming noises. He whistles for the dogs, calls them by name, whistles "Charge!" and does the wolf whistle. Among his many phrases he says: hi, yoo-hoo, go on, get outta here, I love you, he's not here, whew! what? huh? she's a good girl, hello, he's a baby bird, here ya go, see ya later, okay, Larry, Larry Bird, and you're a dingleberry!

African Greys are notorious for saying their phrases at comical and appropriate times. I noticed that frequently when people were at my house, they repeated themselves over and over. Then I noticed that when they were talking, Larry was saying, "What? Huh?" Of course, they probably thought I was deaf as a post. He laughs whenever anyone else laughs. It usually catches people by surprise, which makes them laugh even more, which makes Larry laugh some more. Many times people will all join in laughing, turning red, and wiping tears from their eyes.

One time an important local person was in my house talking to me, when Larry said, "You're a dingleberry, go on, get out of here!" My guest was very surprised because it was my voice and he was not looking at me when it happened, naturally thinking I had said it. I explained that Larry had said it, whereupon we all, Larry included, had a good laugh.

Pawprints on My Heart

A parrot parent has to be careful what she says around her bratty, brainy child. Some workers who were installing blinds asked me how I liked them. Larry looked exactly at where they were pointing and said, "Damn!"

One time, Larry was in the car going to the vet for a check-up. At every light, he did the wolf whistle at the next car. Men and women drivers were looking at me with puzzled, semi-hostile expressions.

When we got to the clinic, the vet opened Larry's carrier and Larry looked up and said "Hello." As the vet went about his examination, he was explaining various tidbits of information about African Greys and their care. Larry would say, "Oh," "Okay," "Huh?" Then the good doctor told me that Larry should have only a few seeds as a treat. Most of the diet should be pellets. Larry looked at him and said, "What? You're a dingleberry." The vet laughed, Larry laughed, and I laughed. As we went out the door, Larry said, "Bye, see ya later."

Whenever Larry's food or water gets low, he yells for me, calling me by name. Over and over he calls out until I have to answer, "What?" "Brenda," he informs me, "you're a dingleberry." Then I fill up his cups, he makes some rather rude "gastrointestinal noises," tastes his food and goes, "Hmmmm, good." Then he says, "Okay, see ya later."

Toria Gaunt

A native of Southern California, Toria Gaunt has been writing since she was ten. She has degrees in theatre, journalism, and law. Her first novel, "Uneven Advantage," is a detective mystery and is scheduled to go to the publisher in the fall of 2000. The second is a young adult mystery and is in the editing stage; the third will be a sequel to the second.

Toria continues to write short fiction and has a collection begun with a working title of "Eccentricities."

In addition to writing, Toria sings tenor with the Chesapeake Chorale and in the choir at Campbell Memorial Presbyterian Church in Weems, Virginia.

Just Jake
by Toria Gaunt

I was nine, or maybe ten, the first time I heard the expression "just jake." I was in the back seat of my neighbor's old Plymouth, the Pepto-Bismol pink one with the ripped seat cushions and cracked window. She pointed to a dog asleep in the grass on a sunny spring day and said, "Life's just jake for that ol' boy."

"Huh?" I asked, stirred from a daydream.

"Just jake, just jake, y'know, cool, okay, right on!" What can I tell you? It was the sixties.

Just Jake

Life was not just jake for the black Labrador I spied padding up a steep hill thirty years later. He was more bones than skin with hips, ribs, and head knot all too prominent. I stopped my pickup, leaned out the window and asked if he was okay. Shrinking from the sound of my voice, he tucked his tail between rear legs and slipped away up an adjoining road.

Two days later I saw him again on the same stretch of road. It was hot and dusty and bits of debris stuck to his coat as cars whizzed by him. His concentration was so pure that he never heard me come up behind him. I pulled over on to a small shoulder and watched. I knew with certainty that if I did not intervene he would starve to death.

I took off for the nearest grocery, so intent on my errand that I didn't notice the wave of a friend going past in the opposite direction. I scoured the shelves in the store for something meaty but with some fat in it too. He needed my mother's beef stew, a rib-sticker if ever there was one, but she had died three years earlier. It struck me then that perhaps it was she who put him in my path.

I snatched a bottle of water from a low shelf and found a can opener. A supply of picnic-type bowls rounded out the fare and I went off in search of my boy.

The sun was just edging below the tree tops and it would be dark soon. I traveled the same road up and back many times but no dog. Tears stung my eyes as I pondered the possibility that he had been hit or worse. My small community had recently hosted a rash of black Lab thefts. The dogs were taken to laboratories where they were the subjects of science experiments.

I came to the same crossroad where I had seen him on the first day and made the turn so sharply that I imagined my little truck balanced on two wheels, movie-style. Up a small incline and to the left I saw what looked to be the now-familiar outline of the dog trailing behind a young woman and a little boy. My heart sank at the thought that he was theirs and just undernourished.

I tried to be calm as I got out of the truck and approached them. He turned at the sound of crunching gravel under my feet and fixed a gorgeous pair of brown eyes on me. Before the woman could answer, I squatted and held out my hand, palm down, for him to sniff. He came over to me, tail wagging in a circle. He nuzzled me with a dry nose. "Hi. Do you belong to him?" I asked, pointing at the Lab.

"No. Someone left him on the road about a month ago. I let him eat out of my scrap pile but I can't afford no dog."

"Mind if I feed him?" I asked, opening the can of food, caring not about her answer but about his need. The tail wag became a full body wriggle as he realized what I was doing. He bumped me with his nose urging me to go faster. I was eye to eye with him and whispered, "Almost there, big boy."

I emptied half the can into a bowl and poured a large quantity of water into another. After finishing his first course he started on the water. I took a fistful of fur and skin to test for dehydration and was shocked at how long it stood up. This boy was in some serious trouble.

I loaded the rest of the can into his empty bowl and he worked on that for a while. I didn't want him to suck down a whole can of dog food and then just throw it up. A thin calico kitten had wandered over and proceeded to get its head stuck in the dog food can. Laughing, I held the can while she pulled herself out, covered in the remains of dog food.

I looked once more at the dog and found that he had lain down on his back giving me his belly in submission. I rubbed it gently as he did a back dance on the grass, turning this way and that, his big ropey tail swishing against my leg.

Although I thought that he was only about six months old at the time of the rescue, the vet told me that he was a year old. A year old and only 42 pounds. He had lost a third of his weight in a month on the road alone. The large scar circling his neck was probably from either being tied up too tight or a collar never loosened when he was a puppy.

It took five months for him to reach his optimum weight of 75 pounds. His once-ragged coat is now glossy and thick, not a bone in sight.

Gazing out the kitchen window on this sunny spring afternoon, I see him asleep on his side in the grass with his constant companion, the calico I named Stuck.

Things are just jake for my Jake.

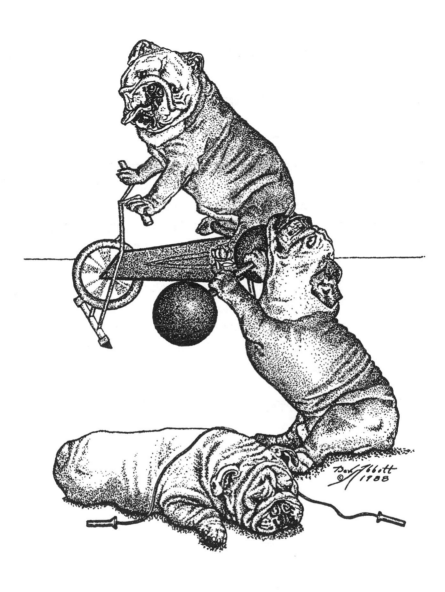

Page 71

Emeline Bailey

Emeline Bailey was born in New Jersey but grew up in Texas. The widow of an Air Force Colonel, she has four children, 7 grandchildren, and two great-grandchildren from that marriage. Her essays have been published frequently in both the *Daily Press* and the *Virginia Gazette*. And for the past 15 years she has served as volunteer and docent at the Thomas Nelson home in Yorktown. Recently married to another writer, Rick Bailey, she now resides in Cobbs Creek where she and Rick host the Mathews Critique Group of the Chesapeake Writers CLub.

How to Handle Males
by Emeline Bailey

Never did I ever dream that I'd spend my golden years on the end of a leash. On the other end is my cherished Shih Tzu. (Do pronounce it 'She-Sue' in my presence. Thank you.) My dog, Luki Plushbottom Wood, is a descendant of Princess Tiger Lily Lotus Blossom and Emperor Ping Pong Confucious. (I didn't make up these names--check out his AKC papers.) Believe me, this little guy is a royal pain in the neck. For instance, he takes me for a walk every day around Surrender Field, except when there's precip falling out of the sky, especially snow. Then he defiantly anchors his feet on the front porch, lowers his head (making him look like Bugs Bunny flattened by a steamroller), and refuses to move, period. Standard equipment on Shi Tzu feet includes powerful suction cups filled with Crazy Glue. Ignoring my blandishments, bribes, and threats, he will not move a micro-freckle. Okay, I admit he can be hoisted up by his adoring coolie slave, me (incidentally, it wouldn't hurt him to lose a few pounds), and then be plunked down on the lawn. Fat lot of good that does. There he stands, in a holding pattern, if you get my drift, doing absolutely nothing but glaring at me with a flagrantly bad attitude until I give up and return him to the house. This behavior makes me as nervous as a little girl bird. If bad weather persists, we may have a problem. Result: I keep my eyes glued on him every second, losing sleep and ruining my disposition until he decides to get with the program.

Kinda reminds me, in a way, of my late husband who could drive from Yorktown to Dallas without having to stop once, unless the car needed something. The kids and I had to make pit stops every thousand miles or so; apparently we weren't equipped with the superior plumbing mechanism possessed by Air Force colonels and Shih Tzus.

There's a heap of difference between a plain dog and a Shih Tzu. Our last dog, Pinto, the offspring of Sophia, an Italian Greyhound and an unknown German Shepherd opportunist, was the happiest, most ebulient dog ever, especially when a member of the family showed up. What a welcome! She'd jump up onto your lap while you were still walking down the driveway. Luki, on the other hand, may or may not bestir himself from his fifth nap of the day to wag his tail lackadaisically when he sees me, even if I've been away two or three weeks. How demoralizing to have a relationship with a laid-back, inscrutable creature of impeccable Chinese ancestry who only recognizes my existence when he's in the vet's office. Then, and only then, he obviously thinks I'm the greatest thing since the invention of wide-angled panty hose.

Luki was absolutely whacko about my now ex-boyfriend. The little creep would run around the house like a dervish and jump up and down in doggie ecstasy as soon as my friend parked in the driveway. Hey, I'm the gal who paid all of Luki's outrageous bills, and that was the thanks I got! And sometimes Luki will tolerate a little bit of lovin', but then sometimes he has a headache. (Why does this also remind me of my husband?)

Admittedly, there are nice things about this breed, such as: (a) Luki sheds hair only in clumps as a result of my grooming him at least twenty-four hours a day; (b) he can't jump over the low barriers erected to keep him off my oriental rugs, his atavistic passion for which goes back to the genes of Emperor Ping Pong (who sounds like a fun guy to me); and (c) because of his short legs, he's unable to get up on the beds and sofas.

Now Pinto loved to take a little nappy-poo on the living room sofa when nobody was home. One day a lady wearing a black wool outfit walked out the front door after a visit. I was appalled to see that her posterior was covered with white and tan dog hair, from stem to stern (and a mighty formidable stern it was, too, I might add). The wool must've contained a blend of Velcro and Scotch tape, sticky side out, which attracted every bit of loose dog hair in the entire house. Wonder if she ever thought about taking a patent out on it?

Sadly enough, Luki's table manners are less than perfect. I've been yelling at him for five years, "Bring your food to your mouth, not your head down to your food, you animal, and for goodness sake, chew with your mouth closed." Luki, my pet, you're beginning to get on my nerves.

I've given up trying to get him to obey any command, suggestion, or prayer on my part unless he jolly well feels like it. He's gotten pretty good at 'sit' when there's a garbage pizza involved. I'm still trying to teach him to roll over on his back and extend his legs straight up in the air in response to 'which would you rather be, married or dead?'

But Luki is so cuddly, after his bath, that is, and when he cocks his head Shih Tzu fashion, protrudes his pouty lower lip, and bats those long eyelashes at me, I realize that he's really got my number, forevermore. So I'll just continue to handle him the way my English friend and I decided is the proper way to treat all male dogs, i.e., determine exactly what it is they want to do and then do everything in one's power to help them do it, which, incidentally, also works quite well with men.

Bev Abbott

Page 77

Rick Bailey

Rick is a former technical writer of computer software documentation; installation and user's manuals supporting satellite control, Apollo spacecraft tracking, naval engineering support, database management installation and operation telecommunication, graphics and financial modeling systems. He has also written over 200 short stories about life that are much stranger than fiction could ever be.

Rick is married, father of two wonderful (grown) children, master to Happy Dog (HD), great uncle to eight nieces/nephews even though he's not old enough to be a great anything! He is a member of the Chesapeake Bay Writers Club, the Mathews Volunteer Rescue Squad, and United We Stand America.

Rick's motto is "It is better to light one candle than to curse the darkness!"

Changes In Life
by Rick Bailey

Changes in life can frequently be very hard to make. Like others, I have made many changes but it was not until recently that I learned about the courage, faith, and trust it sometimes takes to accept the more difficult adjustments in life.

I had spent most of my childhood and much of my adult life in one area, before I finally decided to leave my hometown and follow my dream. By that time I had spent 20 years of my life learning to live in a wheelchair, and I was looking forward to the day when I could build a barrier-free home somewhere in the Tidewater Area. Part of the dream included a small dock and sailboat from which I hoped to sail the far reaches of the Chesapeake Bay and possibly points beyond.

By the time the house was finished, the money I had set aside for the sailboat was also finished, but I felt fortunate to have a pier, a small power skiff, and I finally lived less than 50 feet from the edge of the water. During the summers that followed, my small terrier dog, Happy, and I enjoyed many hours cruising in the skiff, biding our time until a sailboat that would allow extended cruises could be acquired.

Happy had always been terrified of water. Prior to this time, he did not like being even close to water, which was quite evident by the low profile he kept whenever I began just to think about giving him a bath. By his way of thinking I am sure the creek behind our home, not to mention the bay, had to be the biggest bathtub he had ever imagined. To me, it took a giant leap in courage for him to climb aboard the skiff, which he finally managed to do. From that time on he seemed to enjoy the bay almost as much as I did.

One weekend I went down to the pier to ready the skiff for use later that afternoon. Happy followed me as far as the edge of the deck that runs across the back of the house, where he seemed quite content just to sit, basking in the sun and watching from that vantage point overlooking the water.

The skiff was normally berthed above the water by a hoist system attached to the side of the pier. While I was occupied with the business of turning a hand-crank to lower the skiff, I heard a huge splash behind me on the opposite side of the pier! It sounded as if a large turtle had flopped into the water, except that the turtle continued to flounder and thrash.   At first I thought I might have disturbed a large otter that lives at the end of the creek. On many occasions I've heard the otter raising quite a ruckus by the dock as he swims and plays in the water he calls his home.   The skiff was almost lowered into the water, so I released the hand crank and went to the opposite side of the pier to see what was causing the fuss. When I looked over the edge I saw Happy standing in water up to his neck, snorting and sniffing the bank of the creek, desperately trying to get his bearings. I was clearly within his sight but I remained quiet for a moment to see if he would glance my way. His large brown eyes seemed to be quite useless as he stood frozen in place, with his nose raised high sniffing the air. I could not help but laugh, as he stood there soaking wet, looking so helpless and out of place, as I tried to reassure him and called his name: "Hap! What are you doing down there?"

He glanced my way the instant he heard my voice. It was all I could do to hold back the wave of emotions I felt when I realized Happy was almost completely blind! I lay on the pier with my arms stretched as far as I could reach. He was just inches beyond my grasp so I talked to him calmly and coaxed him to take one or two steps toward the sound of my voice so I could retrieve him from the water.

Even though the water was warm and the sun was bright in the sky, Happy began to tremble from the tip of his noise to the end of his tail as soon as I got him out of the water. I wrapped him in my sweatshirt and held him close. I had to laugh again because I could not hold back the feelings that seemed to crest inside of me like a huge wave about to break on the beach. Several months earlier, Happy was diagnosed as diabetic.   Since then I had learned how to control his blood sugar level with diet and injections, but he was losing the sight in both eyes. Cataracts frequently result in terriers who are as far along in life as Happy and his diabetic condition seemed to ensure that blindness would be his fate. When I discussed the cataracts with his veterinarian, I was assured there was nothing I could do to slow their development. He went on to note that retina damage was so common in diabetic dogs that Happy would probably not be a good candidate for surgery.

The only encouraging note was that dogs seem to adapt quite well to blindness. For the last few weeks, I felt certain that Happy's vision was starting to fail but it was easy for me to deny. Happy was so familiar with his surroundings and the routine we have shared over the last nine years that he still seemed to know exactly where he was and where he wanted to go. The only physical change I could observe was the clouding of the lenses over his beautiful brown eyes, and an occasional bump into a chair or stool that was left out of place in the kitchen. Happy seemed to have no trouble finding his way around the inside of the house and his hesitation to go into a dark hallway or to venture far out into the yard to relieve himself at night was also easy for me to ignore. Hoping that he could distinguish between bright and dark, I would turn on the light in the hall or garage to give him a point of reference from which he seemed to manage quite well.

Unfortunately, after he stepped off the pier in broad daylight, I could no longer deny his condition or the fact that the life span of a diabetic animal is diminished substantially. I do not know how much longer Hap will be with me; but I do know I will not forget the courage, faith, and trust he has shown in accepting this difficult change in life.

Note: Happy managed to survive three years to the day, after falling off the pier. During that time he tolerated getting insulin shots twice a day and having both cataracts removed.   During surgery, he immediately lost vision in one eye because the retina became detached; the sight in the remaining eye was eventually lost to glaucoma. During the long holiday weekend three years later, I took Hap to an emergency clinic. He had not   been able to eat. The vet diagnosed cancer of the pancreas. I finally let go of Happy, my wonderful friend and companion of 12 years, on Memorial Day 1997.

Shirley Black

Shirley was born to a farming family in El Dorado Springs, Missouri and grew up in Liberty, Missouri. She has been married forty-seven years to a now-retired professor of biology at William and Mary in Williamsburg, Virginia. She is a doting grandmother to five from her three children. In addition to Tabby, the cat, the household is rounded out to four by a middle-aged Maltese dog. She enjoys hobbies of painting, beading, and playing Mah Jong and dominoes.

Transitions

by Tabby as told to Shirley Black

I guess you never know, from one day to the next, what may happen. One day my life changed and would never be the same again.

For as long as I can remember I lived with My Lady. Most days she went off somewhere, but she always came home in the afternoon. I had the house to myself during her mornings away and I could check out some of the places My Lady didn't like me to be, if I had a mind to. When she came home, she would sit at a table moving a stick along piles of paper, leaving strange marks on them

Transitions

here and there. I usually jumped up on the table and sat on the paper she was marking, just to remind her that I missed her and needed attention. Then she would pet me and scratch me until I drooled slobber all over her and myself.

Then one day she didn't come home. I waited and waited. A lady I had never seen before came and took me from my bed. She took me in a car to the house from hell. She kept me shut up in that house for many days with not one but two dog-beasts. These awful beasts were constantly barking and running at me. I guess they wanted to eat me. I was forced to be ever watchful and stay up high out of their reach. It was hard to find a safe time to grab a bit of food or water. Fortunately, I wasn't very hungry, because they never let me have a moment of peace. When I thought I could take it no more, the lady picked me up and carried me outside, leaving the beasts inside the house.

I began to check out the surroundings. Everywhere I went, the beasts had been there before me. I smelled them and it made me nervous. I prowled further away and their scent grew less. I went to the deck of the house next door, ever so quietly, and peeked in a big see-through door. I saw an old man. I ran to the woods and took cover under a bush. From my cover I watched the house for a long time. It was quiet there. Only the old man and his woman lived there, it seemed. I began to hang out on the deck and watch for them.

There! It was the old woman. She saw me. I gave a pitiful cry and she opened the door. She called to me, petted me and make inquiry of me. I did my best to tell her, "I need a home. I don't know where MY Lady is and I can't live in a home with dog-beasts!"

She said, "You look hungry and thin. Let me get you something to eat."

Pawprints on My Heart

She left the door open so I went in to check out this house. No smell of beasts here. Good!

A few steps down and I was face-to-face with the old man. He said, "Shirley, you can't have that cat in the house. You know that I am ALLERGIC." Whatever that is.

Well, I now live with the old man and woman. They have been easy to train, up to a point. I do have to live outside now, but I can look in at them anytime and they come out to brush me and sit with me and they are very good about feeding and watering me. All I have to do is put a paw upon the see-through door and they come out to check on me.

I feared the winter weather would be too much for me, though my coat was growing thick. But no! The old man made a snuggly bed for me, sheltered from the rain and snow and right beside the see-through door. I feel very close to them. When the days and nights were cold it was still warm in my bed. Toasty warm! They would turn a little red eye on and my bed would get warm.

Also, the old man made a fence to keep the beasts off my deck. It is so funny. When the beasts get out of their house they run over here and bark loudly and say they are "going to eat me."

I'm not worried! They can't get over the fence. I can sit up high on my table and see them coming. I smile at them and they bark wildly. Then the old woman opens the door and they run back to their house.

On the coldest days last winter, the old man put me under the house. That was fun. There were so many places and things to explore and lots of warm spots to sleep.

I guess I'll never see My Lady again, but the old man and woman are nice. We often sit watching each other through the see-through door, the sun warming us all and something inside each of us warming us too.

Erika Lotterhos

Erika is from Minnesota and is presently at the Art Institute of Boston. She and Flambé (who is now a healthy happy seventeen-year-old) showed together quite successfully until Erika went off to College.

Girl

by Flambé as told to Erika Lotterhos

I can feel the frigid crisp of March in Minnesota. The moisture of a thawing barn forms dew droplets on my eyelashes and muzzle. I am content in my freshly mucked stall with crunchy hay to nibble on. There are sweetened oats waiting in my feed bucket. There is little more that a horse could ask for; other than for the obnoxious little barn birds to quiet down. I feel grateful for these simple luxuries that have been provided for me. The only price that I pay for all of this is to allow my new owner to ride me every day. She is a sweet young girl and I do not mind the daily exercise. I know that she is trustworthy and would never harm me. I would never hurt her either.

Ah yes, here she comes now, trudging down the aisle to my stall. She carries my halter and lead in one hand and apples in the other. I am continuously amazed at her fragile little body. She is tall for her age, but very thin. She probably weighs only about as much as a bale of hay. I really like her, but I always feel so large and clumsy around her. I feel like I could break her if I moved just right. I wish she wasn't so small. I wonder if she's being fed as well as I am.

She may be small but at least she knows how to behave around a horse. She practiced quite a bit with schooling horses before she ever thought of approaching a fancy girl like me. I won't put up with sudden movements and other stupid things that unknowing humans do. I appreciate her calm demeanor and gentle manners. She certainly wins points every time she brings treats; she does that just about every time she visits me. She has come to visit quite a bit within the last month or two. I've heard other humans around the barn saying that she is my new owner, my new girl. I like having my own girl.

I love the way that she brushes me; slowly and gently. She uses great care around my face and when she's behind me. Oh, that feels so good when she scratches my neck. It can be so hard to itch yourself on the neck sometimes. She's getting out my bitted bridle now. Ick, eew, nothing worse than cold steel in your mouth. At least she knows how to put it on the right way. Sometimes, I see those poor lesson horses wearing bits so twisted that their tongues are pinched and bleeding. Stupid Homo Sapiens can be so careless sometimes. They forget that if we really wanted, we could have them on the ground so fast they wouldn't know what happened. If these ignorant people think that they have control of us, they're only kidding themselves. I almost pity the stupid ones that call us dumb; those are always the ones that we throw on purpose. My girl respects me though, she is always telling me how pretty and sweet I am. I think it's so cute when she does that.

Off we go into the exercise arena now. This shouldn't take too long because she didn't put a saddle on me. I love it when she rides me bareback; it means she just wants to relax, nice and easy. I can barely even feel her getting on because she is so thin. Her warm legs feel good though; it certainly is chilly in this barn. It seems too early for the birds to be building their nests. They certainly are busy; chirping and swooping, swooping and chirping, how obnoxious.

Now that she has had me walk around for a short while and stretch my legs, she cues me to trot. It feels good to stretch, warms me up. My girl is a good rider; she's keeping a good rhythm with me. This would be great if it weren't for those damned birds. I really wish they would quit.

How can I concentrate on what Girl is asking me to do if those noisy birds keep this up? The only thing worse than barn birds is barn flies. At least it isn't fly season yet. What was that, Girl? Time to walk now. Circle to the left, circle right. Canter? Here we go!

Aarggh! Another damned bird just flew down in front of me! This is just too much to take! Sorry, Girl, but I can't canter with these birds after me right now! I'm going to back up! Oh no! They're behind me too! What am I supposed to do? I think they want to hurt me! Ouch! One of them just pulled on my mane! How dare they use my hair to build their stupid little nest! Maybe if I jump left, no, right! Girl, how can you try to talk calmly to me now with the birds after us! They might want you too!

I don't know what to do! Girl feels like she is afraid too! I wonder if the birds pulled her hair also? Maybe if I kick and jump, hop left, they'll leave me alone! I can't be at this part of the arena! I have to get to the other side now!

Girl

Safe now, I'm at the other end finally; the birds still seem to be over there. Oh dear, where is Girl? She's not on my back; did I drop her? Please God no, there she is. She's at the other end where the birds are. They don't seem to be bothering her though. Thank God those awful birds left her alone.

Why isn't she moving? Maybe I should go over there and find out. Girl, move, please move. Come on, get up. Oh no, don't be hurt, Girl! Get up! Maybe if I nudge her, oops! I'm sorry; I didn't mean to hurt you! Why are you holding your stomach? Did I kick her? What if I kicked her stomach while I was fighting the birds! She's crying and she says it hurts there!

Why is she so pale? She looks like she is about to die! Please don't die Girl! What will they do with me if she dies? I hope they don't sell me; I like Girl's family. Oh no, what If they sell me to a dog food company? What if they sell me to a glue factory? Please be okay, Girl! Please don't die!

Why are you shaking so much? Are you cold? I'll just lay down here next to Girl and keep her warm. I'll wait here with you. I never meant to drop you, Girl, I didn't mean to kick you either. Please be okay. Oh, I hope she'll be all right. We'll just wait right here until someone comes, everything will be all right. I love you Girl, I never meant to harm you.

Page 93

Elizabeth Melton

Born in Oklahoma, Elizabeth Melton has traveled the world with a husband in the foreign service while sharing her family of five children with an assortment of animals. She now resides in Williamsburg, Virginia where she divides her time among volunteer work, twelve grandchildren, and the present canine boss of the household, a miniature poodle named Bonnie.

Miss Bris
Oklahoma's Finest Bristol Cream

Miss Bris was born in 1983 and earned conformation and obedience titles before becoming a therapy dog at schools and a local hospital. When veterinary science remedies could no longer hold in check the discomfort of congestive heart failure, her owner made the painful decision to ease her passing. On Bristol's last day, she walked down the aisle of St. Martin's Episcopal Church, holding her leash in her mouth. She lay down by her mistress' feet on cue. The rector announced that all were invited to a celebration of Bristol's life that afternoon. As the parishioners left the communion rail, they stopped and patted Miss Bris. There wasn't a dry eye in the church. That afternoon, many of Bristol's human friends lay their hands on her as she was given the injection that enabled her to throw off the ties that bound her to Earth.

A Lifetime of Dogs
by Elizabeth Melton

I cannot imagine life without dogs. An independent-spirited Irish Terrier filled my childhood. Michael O'Hara--"Mike" for short--moved with us from Oklahoma to Washington, D.C. during World War II, as we followed my father into the Navy. With no leash laws or encouragement to neuter pets, Mike roamed the Maryland suburbs, and terrier mix puppies soon abounded.

Happily, I married a man who also felt that dogs were essential to human life. For forty-two years we have bounced around the world, welcoming dogs into our hearts and homes.

Our first was Abigail, a long-haired dachshund, who came to spend a weekend, and stayed until her untimely death beneath a milk truck five years later. We were in the Air Force in Germany, and lived in a small village. One day, as Abigail and I took our afternoon walk in the fields, we found a herd of cows approaching, and then surrounding, us. I took Abigail in my arms and ran for home, with the cows in hot pursuit. The mystery was solved when a German bride who replaced us in that village apartment later told us that the farmer who owned the cows came for them every evening accompanied by HIS long-haired dachsie. The herd had mistaken Abigail for their master's dog, and Abigail passed into the folklore of Kempfled an der Nahe.

Back home in the U.S., one day my husband saw advertised as "gift to a good home" an Irish Wolfhound. Our fourth daughter was brand-new, so a 175 pound addition to the family seemed like a great idea. We never regretted that decision. Alf traveled halfway around the world with us. He was a fearsome sight to our Lao neighbors, who called him "Tiger!". This gentle giant, who never needed a leash, died in Vientiane and we buried him under the bougainvilleas. Our grief was eased when we learned that his kennel-mates in the U.S. had all died too, seven or eight years being the normal lifespan for this giant breed.

Tramp chose us at the Paris SPCA. He resembled a border collie, and was very nearly a perfect dog for our family of seven. His only flaw was a pronounced wanderlust. He came to know the western Paris suburbs like the back of his paw. "Bonjour, Madame, J'ai notre chien," became a frequent telephone message. Off I would go, with the toddler in the carseat, to retrieve the escape artist.   We met some very nice French people thanks to Tramp.

In Bangkok, a white miniature/toy poodle came to us as a tiny pup. Her grandfather was a well known figure in local canine society, since he occupied the front window of the vet/grooming shop on the main street, his toenails painted bright red. Josephine Patpong was my shadow for fifteen years, easily transported from her Asian birthplace to Virginia and Houston, Texas.   All poodles are "Josephine" to me.

Shadrach co-existed with Josephine for her last several years. This loving black lab was born in a barn in Croaker, Virginia, and grew up with our last child and only son. After years of being his best friend and duck hunting companion, Shad sent his master off to college, and then transferred his attention to our grandchildren as if he had been bred to support crawling, climbing toddlers.

As our nest emptied, both of children and dogs, a friend, whose work and study schedule had become overwhelming, asked if we could help care for her magnificent golden retriever.   For almost three years, Bristol and I were soul mates. She was a perfect lady, who came into my life at the perfect time.

Magic Hours With Miss Bris
by Elizabeth Melton

She greets my awakening with a smile, offering a sock from the laundry basket, her first gift of the day. She awaits her breakfast, uttering muffled pleas for haste. She devours the meager contents of her bowl with shameless relish and expresses her satisfaction with a genteel belch.

She retrieves the newspaper. Her golden leg feathers float fetchingly as she prances back up the driveway, paper in mouth, to be dropped at my feet. Mission accomplished!

Pawprints on My Heart

She lies near the breakfast table, alert, hoping that a morsel will fall, or a bagel bite or leftover cereal milk will become her portion. It does. Joy!

She heads for the cool tiles of the entry hall for an after-breakfast snooze. Lulled by the hum of machines filled with clothes and dishes, she naps--a brief bracer before taking on the day's responsibilities. She relocates to the bathroom floor to monitor my shower, charitably ignoring my physical defects.

She luxuriates in her morning grooming, striking her show dog pose, nose in the air, eager to receive her fresh bandanna, warm brown eyes saying, "Thank you for making me so beautiful." Ready for whatever the day may bring, she prays that she will be included in all my activities and not hear the fateful words, "See you later, Miss Bris."

She leaps gracefully into the back seat of the car, enchanted to hear, "Come on, Bris." She is my partner at my French lesson *chez* Marcel, or as Meals on Wheels are delivered. She visits with special folks at the convalescent center, honored when somber faces light up or wrinkled hands reach out.

She wags a gracious "Thank you" when given right of entry by friends in Queens Lake, or Skipwith, or on College Terrace, then brazenly vacuums each kitchen and dining room in search of morsels gone astray.

She follows me into the bedroom after lunch for our ten-minute toes-up and snuggles as close to the bed as possible, so we can relax and unwind together. Revitalized, Miss Bris seeks any clue that the magic hour of our walk is at hand.

She is ready. Equipped with leash and tennis ball, this is our time. She moves with an eager golden gait until she reaches the park and the leash comes off. She watches as her ball soars, awaits my nod, then runs, retrieves, gives back, *ad infinitum*. She never tires, darting between trees and shrubs to do what she does best: retrieve, and please.

She promenades on Duke of Gloucester Street, her leash in her mouth, modestly receiving the admiration and applause of all who see her. She endures the pats of tourist hands, wishing they wouldn't. She resists the temptation to chase a cat or a passing squirrel, for to do so would incur (oh, shame) reproof.

She celebrates each homecoming with a treat, later consumes her unvaried dry food, never noticing the lack of variety. She then sprawls on the kitchen floor, cluttering work space between sink and stove, alert to every step of the dinner preparation, hopeful for a careless or charitable castoff tidbit of raw carrot, lettuce heart, cucumber, or (*pièce de résistance*) apple.

She surveys me at dinner, appreciating the conversation and aromas, enthusiastically contemplating the possibility of a leftover morsel. Afterward, she is on pins and needles, ears cocked for the "R" word, rawhide. When she hears it, she rushes to the closet where it is kept, throwing herself body and soul into her Lassie imitation: "It's here, right over here. Come on. I'll show you. Almost there. Yes!"

She seizes her treasure, dives onto her rug, and disappears into gnaw-gnaw land for as long as it takes to devour the rawhide. Another belch, and she takes her ease in front of the fire, a golden pillow tossed on a gray carpet. She exudes an aura of peace and harmony as she regards those she loves with worshipping eyes.

She is exhausted. Having lived each moment of the day to its fullest, she takes her usual spot close by my bed, collapses with a contented sigh, and goes to sleep. Scarcely moving, snoring just a little, she renews herself for the endless possibilities of tomorrow: yet another glorious day.

Debi Davis

Debi has trained her own assistance dogs since 1979, when she lost her legs from vascular disease. Her Border Collies were taught to be "home helpers," long before people with disabilities were legally able to use a "service dog" in public.

Debi's enthusiasm for the abilities of toy-breed service dogs to perform valuable assistance work led her to present programs and demos at toy-breed speciality shows and civic organizations. "A toy breed dog can do most mobility tasks except pulling wheelchairs, opening heavy doors, or performing brace/balance work," says Debi.

Debi has written and published several articles on service dogs, toy breed mobility service dogs, and clicker training. Her articles have appeared in *New Mobility Magazine, The Clicker Journal, The AKC Gazette,* and many other publications. She is also the *AKC Gazette* Papillon breed columnist. Most recently, Debi was highlighted in Ed and Toni Eames' July 1999 *Dog World Magazine* column, "Partners in Independence."

When not writing or presenting programs on service work, Debi assists others in training their own mobility assistance dogs. She is a co-list owner of an internet discussion group for those clicker training their own service dogs, called OC-Assist-Dogs@egroups.com. She is married to high-school mathematics teacher, Tim Loose, and lives in Tucson, Arizona with her three Papillon service dogs.

Service With a Woof and a Smile
by Debi Davis

I'm batty about service dogs. Besotted. Addicted. I love training them, writing about them, and sharing smiles about the ups and downs of living life with a twenty-four hour a day canine sidekick.

My service dog's call name is "Peek", short for "Peekaboo." He's a 10 pound Papillon who does the work of a much larger dog. Since I'm severely disabled and work from a wheelchair, Peek's job is to do everything I can't do on my own. Bending over causes me to become very dizzy, so those lower level chores Peek performs give me amazing independence.

What kind of things can a 10 pound puffball do for a person with a disability? Well, he makes my bed each morning, puts clothes in and takes clothes out of the dryer, picks up things I drop, brings me the phone or the TV controls, and opens and shuts cupboard doors and drawers for me. From my lap, he activates light switches, power door openers, elevator buttons. When my manual wheelchair rolls away, he fetches it back to me. He's my butler, my maid, my elevator operator, and my best friend.

What's amazing about Peek, though, is not the amount of work he can do for his diminutive size, but that he was once a dog with so many behavioral problems that he was nearly on death row. A commercially bred Papillon, this little boy had "bobbles" that seemed impossible to change. He was a manic barker, exhibited fear aggression around other animals and human males, and was a snarly resource guarder.

But, through gentle clicker training, he turned totally around, and became a well-adjusted, happy dog who now licks the hands of men when he's doing his therapy work in hospices, and who meets and greets other dogs without as much as lifting his lip. He no longer barks at everything, and allows anyone--even other dogs and the cat--to take treasured bones away from him. He traveled "The Clicker Mile" and was reprieved.

He made the transition so well that he was awarded the highest honor in the service dog world in 1999, winning the Delta Society Beyond Limits National Service Dog of the Year Award, the first time in history a toy breed dog had ever won.

Our journey to Service Dog of the Year was not without its share of funny moments. When Peek was newly certified, I took him to a craft store to do a bit of shopping.

Pawprints on My Heart

Busy looking at all the art supplies on the shelves, I wasn't paying attention to my partner. I brought my purchases up to the counter, and the cashier began scanning them.

The cashier pauses, says, "Ma'am, I see your service dog has your last item. I'll be glad to scan it now." Last item? I'd already placed the last item on the counter. I look down, see Peek with a white rabbit pelt in his chops, holding on to it for dear life.

I'm not about to admit my service dog has just been shoplifting, so I try to cover, and say, "Oh, thank you! I missed that one." I reach down for the pelt, cueing Peek to release. He's clearly not thrilled to hand over his booty to me, but he does respond to the cue. I pick up the pelt, dripping with thick, ropy drool, and place it gingerly on the counter with two fingers. I wipe my fingers on my shorts and look up at the cashier, who quips, "Uh, that's okay. I don't have to scan it. And you can go ahead and give it back to your service dog to carry. I don't want it to get the other items in the bag all wet."

The following week, Peek and I are at the Papillon National Specialty, where we've been asked to do a service dog demo. Our presentation takes place in a carpeted hotel ballroom, right after three days of conformation judging. The carpet is thick with the remains of food treats of all kinds, and is also saturated with tons of marvelously succulent animal smells.

I send Peek out to retrieve the phone for me, and watch horrified as he drops the phone en route back to me, following a scent trail around the ring, scarfing up hot dog bits, pieces of liver, cheese, chicken, and prime rib. I repeat my cue more emphatically, "Peek, fetch phone!"

Peek looks up at me innocently, grabs the phone and begins to trot enthusiastically toward me. He's broadsided by yet another incredibly distracting smell, drops the phone, and wanders off following the trail. I can hear his mind working. "Oh man, look at this liver! Hey--here's garlic turkey. Oh, is this really prime rib? Hey! That cute little female in season parked her fanny right here. I'd better mark it. "

During another demo, Peek is pulling my manual lightweight wheelchair to me, which he does by grabbing on to a leather strap stretched across the front of the chair. He's backing up, pulling the chair to me, when all of a sudden he spots a dog going into the elevator and stops, freezes.

There are 400 Papillons at this speciality show and three or four pets of other breeds in the hotel. The dog entering the elevator with its owner is NOT a Papillon, and Peek lets the world know. WOOF! WOOOOOF! His voice echoes off the marble walls of the hotel lobby, and I shrink to Lilliputian size, wishing I could become invisible.

Life with a service dog also has its deliciously comic moments. Once, while shopping with a friend who uses a Border Collie as a service dog, we're stopped by a shopper who asks, "Are these dogs the same breed?" Although both dogs are black and white with similar markings and coat, Peek is 10 pounds and the Border Collie is 55 pounds. I reply, "Yes, they are actually from the same litter, but this little one shrunk when he got caught with the clothes in the dryer one day. " I expect a laugh, but the shopper takes me seriously!

One day I enter a restaurant with another friend and her white German Shepherd service dog. Both of our dogs do mobility service work. A little girl looks at our dogs, and says to her mother, "Mommy, there's some 'Hearing Eye' doggies!" The mother corrects her, and explains, "They aren't Hearing Eye dogs, honey, those are Seeing Ear dogs. "

A friend of mine took her service dog through a clicker trick training class. The dog's favorite trick was

"ACHOO!"--where the owner sneezes, cueing the dog to pull a hankie out of the owner's pocket and give it to the owner.

One evening they are at a very elegant function, eating dinner at a table resplendent with white linen and crystal. Her service dog is quietly lying under the table, out of sight. During dinner, the owner sneezes, and unbeknownst to her, the dog quietly rises, moves down the length of the table until he finds an open purse with a lovely lace hankie inside it. Of course, he pilfers the hankie and takes it proudly back to his owner!

Another friend of mine uses a guide dog. Waiting for a light to change at a crosswalk, he cues his dog to "forward." But his dog is busy sniffing the light post, and checking pee-mail. My friend restates the cue emphatically, "FORWARD!" The dog still is intent on sniffing and pays no attention. Finally, he shouts in a commanding voice, "FORWARD!" The dog finally responds and begins leading him across the street.

At the corner, he hears two elderly ladies chatting, and one says to the other, "Oh, Sadie. Isn't that the saddest thing you ever saw? A blind man with a deaf dog."

Being partnered with a service dog has its moments of mirth and its moments of great poignancy. Many times when Peek is just doing his normal job, such as picking up my keys in a restaurant, people's eyes will mist over, and they'll say, "Oh, that's the most wonderful thing I have ever seen."

It is very gratifying to know that people can see what a marvelous help these dogs are to those of us who live with disabilities. Unfortunately, I usually get all teary-eyed too, and we human strangers exchange hugs while the service dog sneaks a treat off the floor. Hey, they are STILL dogs!

Diana Gwynne Swenson

Diana is a Jersey gal with a strong southern heritage and a love for felines, especially Ralph who had an almost purr-fect purr-sonality. Her life-long project seems to be to write a story about her adventure trip in Africa.

The First Thanksgiving
by Diana Gwynne Swenson

We decided to take Ralph back to New York with us in the last days of summer. His previous people just had too many animals, especially kittens. Ralph was about three months old and needed a home. Luckily, we were catless at the time. It was love at first sight when we saw the feisty little yellow fellow busily tearing up a phone book.

Ralphie had a most charming personality. However, we decided he wasn't awfully bright because he had acquired a candle-sniffing habit. It wouldn't have been so bad except he always waited until they were lit.

The First Thanksgiving

Thanksgiving was fast approaching and since no special invitations had been forthcoming we planned to take the four-day holiday and return to Virginia, having never even stayed in our new house. My idea was to go to Williamsburg for Thanksgiving dinner--WRONG! It was strongly suggested to me that I do a traditional dinner so that there would be leftovers for the remainder of the holiday weekend. As for myself, I had always hated seeing that picked-over carcass every time I opened the refrigerator.

We managed to get all the right stuff together and I got very housewifely and involved with my cooking chores. The small dining table was opened and placed against the wall. I set it in a holiday mode, complete with center decoration and special wineglasses. My husband carved the turkey and we brought in the vegetables, cranberries, and an opened bottle of port. I had just stepped back to the kitchen when World War III broke out.

NO! NO! DOWN, Ralph! Then Crash--Boom--Bang!!!

Apparently, the aroma of the freshly cooked turkey had overcome him. I ran back in time to see a wild-eyed Ralph clutching the placemat as he and the place setting tumbled to the floor. The cranberry dish had already splattered against the white wall, leaving quite an interesting red pattern. Wine seemed to be flowing everywhere. My immediate thought was "Kill the Cat!" Too late! There was nothing to do except laugh. Ralph couldn't seem to figure out what was going on.

As we came to our senses, we realized we needed to do some fast cleaning up. The wall had to be washed, the table was a disaster, and the rug wasn't looking any too good either.

Almost an hour later, we sat down. Ralph got his own plate. Turned out he didn't care for cranberries very much, but he sure had a passion for turkey. So thereafter if we needed to leave him for any length of time, I would roast a turkey. As it defrosted he would sit silent sentry next to it.

There have been many Thanksgivings since then, most more social, but I remember none of them as vividly as what we now refer to as "Ralph Cranberries" day.

Jean McClellan

Jean McClellan is an alumna of the University of Virginia and a retired registered nurse who is an inveterate people and creature watcher. She is married to a retired internist and counts among her many friends as many four-legged ones as bipeds. She and husband Jason have two grown children and one granddog. A young kitten now keeps them company while they birdwatch. Jean has published numerous stories and articles in local papers and magazines.

Bobby's Tail
(or the Lack Thereof)
by Jean McClellan

"Go wan, get outta here! We don't need any more cats! Besides, you're ugly--you don't even have a tail!" This verbal explosion from the back yard brought me to the door in time to see a streak of buff-colored fur leap into the bayberry bushes, barely escaping the spray from a garden hose brandished by my husband.

Creature lover that I am, this suggestion of mistreatment brought out the mother tiger in me.

Bobby's Tail

"Stop that, you big bully," I yelled. "What did that poor little kitty ever do to you?"

Startled by this challenge, Jason turned off the water, but reaffirmed his position. "Well, we don't need any more cats, and he is ugly!"

I peered into the shade of the bayberry and met two big saucer eyes staring back, one gold, and one brown.

"Come on, fella, let's have a better look at you." The cat, sensing a friend, cut loose with a 25 horsepower purr and sidled slowly forward, careful to keep me between him and the source of the water. My nurturing nature sprang to attention.

"Oh, the poor thing, he's half starved. He's been fighting a lot--look at the size of his jaw muscles; his front end is bigger than his back end, but he has a cute little bunny-tail."

Refusing to be distracted, Jason retorted, "He's ugly! And don't feed him or we'll never get rid of him!"

"I certainly will feed him! And I bet Ginny would like to have him."

Our neighbor's twenty year old cat had recently died, and she responded promptly to an invitation to check out the newcomer. She sat down on the back steps, called the cat, and he came to her with little hesitation. But when she stood up to leave with him in her arms, he stiffened and jumped down.

"Tell you what, Ginny--I'll bring him over first thing tomorrow, and you can start feeding him at your house. He'll stay where the food is."

Next morning, the cat seemed completely agreeable to the idea. He let me carry him across the street, purring all the way. I put him down on Ginny's porch. Confident that our problem was solved, I hurried away. But when I reached our back yard, the cat was already sitting on the steps with a puzzled look on his face.

As several more similar attempts over the next several days proved equally unsuccessful, we were forced to accept that the cat had made up his mind where he intended to live and we were not likely to change it. In spite of our two resident cats spitting and hissing at the sight of him; in spite of Jason's edict, "He stays outside, " the cat was undaunted. So I named him Bobby, and made an appointment with our vet for him for a check-up and a personality change.

While I was planning Bobby's near future, it came to me that maybe Jason didn't like this cat because he still missed Tommy. Tommy was our daughter's kitten, but he grew into Jason's cat. Although he continued to play enthusiastically with Judy, he would follow Jason closely as he worked in the yard, as if supervising the work of his estate. Inside the house, when Jason would get up from his favorite chair, Tommy would jump into it, yawn widely, and sit tall with an air of authority. Jason dubbed him "The Regal Rascal." Tommy had a sixth sense about Jason's arrival home. He would be sunning himself on the back steps and suddenly jump up and go racing around to the front of the house. When Jason pulled into the driveway, Tommy would be sitting on the walk washing his face in apparent boredom. He would look up as if to say, "Oh, its you again." He would then turn and precede Jason up the walk to the front door, meowing all the way. We gave him an imaginary script.

"As long as you're here, you can open the door for me--I can't reach the door knob; it must be nearly time for dinner, don't you think? And by the way, how was your day?" (Tommy had met his demise about two years before Bobby appeared.)

As Bobby's hormone titer went down, his big jaw muscles diminished and the rest of his body filled out until his bow and stern were better balanced. He was really becoming almost handsome.

One day, Jason had been working in the yard and came inside for a coke, with Bobby following close on his heels.

"Wait a minute," I said. "Didn't you decree that Bobby was to be an outside cat?"

Pretending not to know he had been followed, Jason said, "Well, I guess we could watch him and see how he behaves."

So help me, Bobby winked his brown eye at me, yawned widely and sat taller with an air of authority. The familiar pose was startling.

"You know what? I think this is Tommy come back without a tail so he could be more like you!" Jason pretended not to hear.

The next day, we arrived home together and there sat Bobby on the front walk, washing his face in apparent boredom. He looked up at Jason as if to say, "Oh, so it's you again." He then turned and preceded us up the walk, meowing all the way.

"As long as you're here, you can open the door for me--I can't reach the door knob; it must be nearly time for dinner, don't you think? And by the way, how was your day?"

John W. Dayton

John Dayton, 73 as of the millenium, was educated in Teaneck, New Jersey public schools, Mount Hermon Prep, and The College of William and Mary. In mid-career (US Foreign Service), the State Department sent him to Cornell for 18 months of graduate schooling in Southeast Asian Studies. As a diplomat he served three- to five-year tours in Amman, Mogadiscio, Djarkarta, and Tokyo, and a five-year retirement tour at Camp Peary as chief of senior officers training courses. After retiring in 1980, he built an earth-sheltered solar house in Williamsburg, did community volunteer jobs, and then, in 1984, joined the development office at W&M, for which he traveled and raised money for the next fifteen years. Now "retired" again, he provides pro-bono fund-raising advice to a number of charitable causes and serves as chair of the Annual Fund at W&M's Virginia Institute of Marine Science. He and his wife Julie have "always" had much-loved animal companions-- dozens over the years--but the Elkhound/Lab, Moonshine, and a Himalayan named Sunji will forever have special places in their garden and in their hearts.

Moonshine

by John W. Dayton

Moonshine was born on the campus of Amherst College in August 1978, the result of a romantic but ill-advised dalliance between a beautiful Norwegian elkhound and a raffish, traveling black Labrador. She spent her infant year in son Win's fraternity house, cadging beer and pretzels and became a party animal forever after--a party animal with webbed feet, a double coat, and the Lab's affable personality.

She came to Virginia on Win's graduation and spent her youth at Camp Peary, where she had important

Moonshine

duties. Each dawn and dusk a herd of deer would appear in the meadow in front of our house. The turf was clearly hers. She would charge forth to drive them off with lusty barks and much tail-wagging. The deer were never in any serious danger.

After a time, she would return enormously pleased, and expect thankful pats and congratulations for her success in driving away these dangerous interlopers. She also had to explore every nook and cranny of the base, and in the process, she met several handsome, small animals with black, furry coats and white stripes down the middle of their backs. She brought home unmistakable evidence of these encounters and never understood why we found her new playmates so objectionable. The bill for tomato juice was staggering.

In 1980, at retirement time, Moonshine moved to Williamsburg and lived for a year on Lake Powell Road and then for a few months at Grandma's house on Newport Avenue. During this year, she supervised the construction of the house in Kingspoint. The bulldozer operator had to be watched carefully, the cement truck had to be given guidance, and every arriving load of lumber and supplies had to be checked in.

During construction, Moonshine enjoyed the companionship of a large, black standard poodle, Grendel Schmidt, who lived up the street. The two chased each other over and around the fresh mountains of bulldozed earth with endless enthusiasm. Finally, thanks to Moonshine's careful attention, the architect's plans were implemented to her satisfaction and we moved in.

For the next nine years, Moonshine shared her life with the fortunate human she chose to live with. We shared some good times and bad, but throughout, she was my constant companion and friend. She was also the main security for the house, but her most important role was that of meeter-and-greeter and hostess extraordinaire.

No guest could arrive without a gracious welcome by Moonshine. No cocktail or dinner party was complete without her. She was far too dignified to beg, but somehow she seemed to acquire her share of hors d'ouevres.

She also had an important educational role. Each newborn or new-on-the-block infant eventually met Moonshine and learned that a fearsome, black beast with glistening fangs could also have soft brown eyes and a pink velvet tongue that slurped. She had eminently pullable ears and tail and a shaggy coat just right for tiny fingers to clutch for support.

As we both got older and smarter, we began to walk for our health. Brisk two-mile aerobic hikes three or four times a week around the eastern quadrant of Kingspoint because our routine. As the years went by, Moonshine began to lag, and toward the end, she was unable to keep up. I could tell how much it hurt her to have to sit in the middle of the road and admit that she couldn't go on.

I knew she had arthritis and suspected there might be other difficulties. I checked her in to the veterinary hospital. After tests the news was not good, and after her additional weekend in the hospital, the vets let me know that there was simply no hope. We could keep Moonshine alive a few more weeks, perhaps a few more months, but the quality of her life would only get worse. Knowing what had to be done, I asked the vet that it be done at home. He brought her home about noon in his pickup.

She had to be helped from the truck but she walked straight through the house and out onto the deck where I had planned for us to part. The spot she favored most in good weather was at the edge of the deck, where she could rest her chin on the lower railing while surveying her domain, the marsh at the confluence of the two creeks and the loveliest view in Williamsburg.

Kindly, the doctor and I sat down beside her, and I scratched her ears and stroked her muzzle the way she especially liked. I don't think the gentle lethal shot was painful, and the patient, resigned expression on Moonshine's face seemed to say, "I know you mean well."

The velvet tongue gave me one last slurp and then, with a deep sigh, she put her head down and went to sleep. It was the first really cool, crisp day of autumn and a soft breeze ruffled her coat. She was the most amiable friend I ever had.

A neighbor's child asked me if doggies go to heaven. I had given some thought to that myself; like a good Episcopalian, I fudged. I said that while we can never know God's plans and intentions exactly, we can be sure that he will always do what's best for all his creatures.

Privately, I am persuaded that somewhere there is a big, shaggy, black, joyfully barking, tail-wagging dog chasing an endless herd of prancing deer across a sun-slashed meadow.

And though she never tires, I think this dog at the end of the day finds a deck with a beautiful view and a lower railing at just the right height for her chin. And maybe some day, if I am lucky, I will be there with her.

Page 123

Justina Carlson

Since 1984 Justina Carlson has lived in 17 countries outside the USA for a total of 66 months. While her husband of 34 years does his "research mathematics," she enjoys the adventure of adapting to other cultures and trying to learn their languages. A life-long pet owner, it is only recently that she has been taking her two papillons, Maki and Gigi, with her on these excursions.

Her background is in Christian Education and writing. She enjoys teaching, story telling, studying Biblical history, gourmet cooking, entertaining, and photography. On occasion, she can be persuaded to don her clown costume and assume her alter ego, Miss Hap.

More Than a Pet
by Justina Carlson

Faithful companion,
Clown ambassador of
Gentleness and good will.

Sheer joy of being that
Fed and enriched us --
Delightful symbiosis.

Untimely wrenching --
Living memories heal
The gaping wound.

Forever endures
Far longer than years

Linda Collins Reilly

Linda Collins Reilly was born in northern New Jersey and grew up there, nurtured by many dogs and cats. She has degrees from Vassar College and The Johns Hopkins University, and she moved to Williamsburg, VA in 1969. From that time until the present Linda has taught classics and archaeology at William and Mary. She began to breed and show Akitas in the 1970s, and switched to Pembroke Welsh Corgis in 1981. She has shared her life with many Corgis, including Rumpus, born profoundly deaf. Linda presently has three Pems, Tickle, Dash, and Pink, the latter two of her own breeding. Even though the three Corgis are grandmother, mother, and daughter, they have three very distinct personalities, which she has tried to capture here with this short haiku.

Corgi Haiku
by Linda Collins Reilly

the sweetest dog
angel in a fur suit
Tickle

brave and bold
brilliant dark eyes shine fire
Dash

run! a joyous bark!
little white feet fly!
Pink

Dot Bryant

Born in Roanoke, Virginia, Dot came to Williamsburg to attend William and Mary as a freshman. Forty-three years and two degrees later, she is still in Williamsburg. After working for the Commonwealth of Virginia in higher education for 28 years, Dot retired and went to work at the National Center for State Courts. She and her husband Bill are hard core cat people, but have also owned several dogs over the years.

Dot's main interests are her four grandchildren (who also live in Williamsburg), gardening, reading, and working jigsaw puzzles.

Two Cats

by Dot Bryant

One day a co-worker arrived at the office with some kittens in a box. They were the offspring of a stray cat who lived on her property but who would not be caught. When the kittens were old enough to be weaned but still tiny, a ferocious rain storm swept through the area. As my co-worker's husband ran toward the house, he saw one of the kittens in a hole filled with rain water, desperately trying to claw his way out. The husband rescued him, took him inside, dried him out and gave him some dinner. The next day, after capturing the other kittens, my co-worker took them to work to find homes.

"A cat with a story," I said. "I like that." So I named the tiny black and white fuzz-ball Duke of Gloucester (after the county where he was born and almost died) and took him home.

Duke was a delightful kitten (aren't they all?) and as he grew he developed three distinct personas. One was "Duke the Jungle Cat," who would hide under the skirt of the couch and wait for one of the other cats to walk by. His paw would snake out and smack the unsuspecting cat who would leap several feet into the air, land ungracefully, and look around for the ambusher who would of course be invisible.

The second persona was "Duke the Grizzly Cat." One of Duke's main joys in his young life was to capture my arm, wrap his legs around it, and gnaw on my hand. He especially enjoyed standing on his hind legs, with his front legs wrapped around my arm, gnawing away--as we imagined grizzly bears probably do.

But the most entertaining persona was "Duke the Retriever Cat." He loved carrying things around the house in his mouth, his favorite being a skein of yarn. He knew where the basket of yarn was and he'd often choose a skein of an appealing color and carry it in his mouth, trotting purposely from room to room with the yarn dragging between his legs, tripping him at every other step. My husband Bill and I speculated about what might be going on in his little brain, but soon gave that up! His career as a retriever culminated in an incident when he was home alone. He had chosen a skein of yarn, brought it into the den where he somehow managed to anchor a loose end of it to a piece of furniture. He then proceeded to carry his unwieldy burden around the center wall of the house, through corners of the kitchen and dining room, down the length of the living room, around the end of the hall, and back through the den, unraveling and wrapping the yarn as he went--not one, or twice, but seven times! He was on his eighth circuit when Bill came home. Instinctively, Duke imagined that what he was doing was not a good thing, so he abandoned the job, ran away, and hid in a closet. Bill's response was, of course, disbelief and laughter. After that day, however, Duke seemed to lose interest in yarn wrapping. He retained his other personas, however, and continued to entertain and delight us. Unfortunately and inexplicably, he began to fear many things, especially the grandchildren whose arrival in the house was greeted with bewildered horror by Duke.

When Duke was about two years old, Bill came home from the vet's office one day with another tiny black and white fluff ball. This one also was part of a litter born to a homeless cat, captured and brought in by a caring person. We watched our new acquisition as he did all the usual kittenly things, but with style and exceptional aggression. His wicked personality shone in his face, so we unfortunately gave him a name he became determined to live up to--Hagar the Horrible.

When he was only a few months old, he suddenly disappeared one day. We searched our neighborhood and the surrounding vicinity all day, but could not find him. Late that night, I was awakened from fitful sleep by frantic scratching at the front door. Hagar had come home and wanted to tell us about his adventures. Bill and I had to sit in our usual places in the living room while Hagar paced back and forth on the end table between us, describing his day of wandering and encountering all manner of dangerous creatures and events. After that, he was content to stay mostly in our yard.

Two Cats

Hagar the Horrible soon became an amazing mix of drooling affection and vicious mauling. When he made that special trip to the vet that all young male cats have to endure, we hoped that his personality and behavior would change--and these things happened--sort of--he began to give fair warning by a loud "YEEOOWW!" before biting me or Bill or the children or the dog or whoever was nearest. I stoutly defended him for many years ("He's just a baby!") until he finally began to mellow and would quite often allow himself to be stroked without turning into Mr. Hyde-cat.

Hagar is a most companionable fur person, accompanying me in the yard hanging up the laundry or weeding the flowerbeds. He is always in the middle of everything, sleeping peacefully in the living room floor, while the four grandchildren dash and jump around him, barely missing him with their doll strollers and shopping carts or covering him with Barbie dolls and Beanies. His favorite play-toy was the Rottweiler and they were good friends until Bear's recent death.

When he was a tiny kitten, Hagar delighted in ambushing Duke, who patiently endured and often seemed to enjoy their encounters. As Hagar matured, he and Duke established a rather distant but cordial relationship, greeting each other with deferential head-licking. He treats the old and frail cat Pudd'n with respect and restraint, probably realizing that she offers little sport.

Such is life with our two fluffy black and white elegant and fascinating cats, our companions, friends, entertainment, and comfort. We treasure them, photograph them, carry on conversations with them, and refuse to imagine life without these two fur people.

The Rottweiler Who Thought He Was a Pussycat

By Dot Bryant

We first met Bear when our son brought him from DC to visit us in Williamsburg. Bear was about six months old, but was several times the size of Hagar the Horrible, our full-grown fluffy black and white cat. Bear, who was totally unacquainted with even the concept of cats, came bounding in the house, not yet aware that he was a fearsome Rottweiler. He saw the cat on a chair under the dining room table and bounced forward to make friends.

The Rottweiler Who Thought He Was a Pussycat

Slash, slash, went Hagar's claws and yip, yip, went Bear, backing off more in confusion than pain. Hagar had a bath while Bear sat down to think it over.

Thus began a friendship of many years as Bear first visited us occasionally and finally came to live with us for good. Bear still did not know he was a Rottweiler, so he and Hagar spent many hours playing, lunging, barking or yowling, and entertaining us immensely. Sometimes Hagar would hook his claws into Bear's conveniently loose jowls and Bear would shake his huge concrete head from side to side, giving Hagar a sort of roller coaster ride. At other times, Bear would come upon Hagar peacefully sleeping in the middle of the living room floor (chosen, of course, in true catly fashion for maximum inconvenience to the rest of the family). Slipping his nose under Hagar's belly, Bear would flip him up and over, like a fluffy soccer ball. Occasionally, a little blood would appear, always on Bear's face, but he never seemed to mind. When they tired of playing, they would curl into half moons, the tops of their heads touching, and nap for a while.

As the two grew older, their play became less strenuous, but their friendship continued, as they napped together with either heads or rumps joined. Even through the last three years of Bear's life, after he was diagnosed with diabetes, they remained gentle companions, with Hagar winding around Bear's hugs paws and Bear nudging and sniffing Hagar until they settled down for a nap. Bear learned to purr from Hagar. He would come to me, butt me with his head, and growl softly as I petted him. We sometimes growled in unison, increasing the volume until others in the vicinity lost patience.

There were occasional differences of opinion between Bear and the humans of the household, primarily over turf and over any belongings of our son which were left lying around the house. Bear's devotion and loyalty to his first human friend remained constant and his guard dog instincts would surface whenever he felt required to guard a boot or a t-shirt from dangerous marauding enemies, such as my elderly mother trying to get into the bathroom or my brother trying to sleep on the couch. The results of these differences of opinion were usually a stern order from the humans and much grumbling from Bear as he obediently but reluctantly left the room. These episodes of guard dog behavior clearly revealed a pussycat in a Rottweiler suit.

Bear was also a gentle companion to the grandchildren, who sat on him and hugged him and dressed him in various hats and scarves. Whenever any of the children spent the night with us, Bear would insist on sleeping on the floor between the twin beds, snoring mightily, but doing his duty of guarding the possessions of his favorite human.

Life with Bear was not always fun, however. I'll always remember painfully the morning when I was rushing to get out of the house to work before dawn. The combination of a dark room, a dark green rug, and a black cement dog resulted in a nasty break of my arm near the shoulder and months of unpleasant physical therapy. The image of myself lying on the floor screaming, with coffee dripping everywhere, and Bear interrupting his sleep only to lift his head and blink his eyes a few times, is rather amusing now, three years later.

In his last years, Bear remained a gentle friendly house dog, who welcomed with messy affection all who entered the house, leaning lovingly against friends and strangers alike, tail stump vibrating madly. He continued his friendship with Hagar, his deference to the ancient and frail cat Pudd'n, and his curious but mercifully distant attention to the timid cat Duke who was afraid of everything. After he left us at the age of 10½, my brother

The Rottweiler Who Thought He Was a Pussycat

summed up his life: "He was a good old dog and I don't think anyone ever told him what a vicious and fearsome breed he belonged to."

Page 137

Kathy Godfrey

Born in Ohio, Kathy has lived in North Carolina for the past 13 years. She has worked for 30 years as an educator, and is a school administrator in Raleigh. She has a grown daughter who is a chemical engineer. Kathy is currently working on a doctoral degree at North Carolina State University. She enjoys volunteer work, the beach, gardening, reading and writing, collecting vegetarian receipes, and animals. Her first Papillon died suddenly at only four years of age. Tutu's abrupt death at such a young age was a terrible blow, but Kathy memorialized her with the story that follows and by adopting another tiny black-and-white Papillon from the Papillon Club of America's rescue committee. Spring, now renamed Bijou (French for jewel), is helping to fill the void in the house left by the vibrant little presence of Kathy's much loved Tutu.

Astra's Picture Perfect (aka Tutu)
June 21, 1996 - July 22, 2000

Beloved companion, friend, and soulmate of Kathy, Tutu was a show dog early in her life, but was retired because of her tiny size. She was a fun Papillon! She loved many things: the beach; her cousin Priss and Priss' human Carolyn; squeaky toys; playing tug, hide and seek, and chase; walking outside; meeting new people; eating; being brushed; sleeping with Kathy; going to school with all the children; riding in her car seat; and running errands.

Tutu
by Kathy Godfrey

I enjoy the home town advantage of living in Raleigh, North Carolina, the location of a series of eight dog shows held each spring on consecutive days and called the Tar Heel Circuit. My friend Carolyn and I treated ourselves to a relaxing Saturday in the spring of 1997 and found ourselves at the side of the Papillon ring. That was my first meeting with Tutu.

This little black-and-white charmer was beginning her show career at this group of shows, strutting around the ring in puppy class and more or less minding her handler. Her older sister took the points, but Tutu captured my heart that day. The handler and her mother were friendly and responsive to my questions, allowing me to hold little Tutu after she finished showing. I was convinced that I wanted to get a little Papillon to share my life after meeting this beguiling little minx. It was not long before I called the breeder, whose name was given to me by Tutu's handler, to ask about adoption procedures and availability of puppies.

I hoped for a puppy that would resemble the one I'd met that first day, so I was overjoyed when the breeder called in late summer to say that Tutu's tiny size made her unsuitable for breeding and therefore she would be available to me as a pet.

I would later learn that I'd had competition as a possible companion and had been chosen for little Tutu because my high-energy personality matched Tutu's so perfectly. And match it did. We were soul mates who did everything together with glee. She was entertainment, laughter, companion at home and at work. She was dubbed the Assistant to the Assistant Principal by the children at school, often sitting in my office under the desk or making points with the children with a wag of her tail or a flick of her large butterfly ears.

I was constantly amazed and entertained by her accomplishments despite her tiny size. One fall morning comes vividly to mind. Snuggled under the warm blankets, I was sleeping peacefully when – surprise! clunk! – something hard hit my face. My mind was jolted awake, my ears listened intently, and my eyes peered cautiously into the early light of dawn. Hearing nothing, my mind and eyes tried to determine what had fallen on me. As my eyes adjusted to the morning light and my brain sorted out the situation, I realized Tutu was staring at me. Lying right beside my face was her small food bowl.

"What do you want?" I asked.

Tutu whined and nudged at the bowl with her nose.

"Are you hungry?"

Tutu wagged her tail and licked her lips.

I got up and fixed Tutu's breakfast, all the while wondering how she jumped up on the bed with the food bowl in her mouth.

Not that jumping was out of the ordinary for Tutu. I had taught her to be my Pap-on-lap. Dr. Seuss had his Pop-on-Top and I had my Pap-on-Lap. I would say that and she would jump up on my lap. The children loved it, especially when we were studying Dr. Seuss.

And Tutu would routinely bring me the bowl when she was hungry, so her bringing the bowl was not surprising. Jumping on the bed was routine, too, although it usually took two or three attempts for her little legs. Surprising and unexplained is how both she and the bowl got up on the bed that morning without waking me up.

Some months after Tutu came to be my soul mate, my friend Carolyn lost her aging canine friend. After much thought, she decided she wanted a Papillon in her own life also. That is how Tutu's first cousin Priss came to join our happy band. Priss was as laid-back as my friend Carolyn, much different from Tutu in energy and expression, but as well matched to Carolyn as Tutu was to me. The four of us shared many adventures together, especially vacations at the beach.

And then suddenly and unexpectedly, Tutu was gone. We went out to feed the birds, our morning ritual. Then Tutu curled in her bed under my computer to sleep while I went through my usual Saturday morning efforts of reading computer mail and planning my day. When I went to take clothes out of the dryer, she didn't follow me. I was curious at the departure from routine but not alarmed until she didn't come at my call. I rushed back to my desk to find her with

Tutu

blood in her eyes and nearly lifeless under my desk. A frantic rush to the nearest vet proved useless; she was gone before I could reach his office.

I miss her terribly. She was such a special little girl. Many people at school cried when I told them of her passing. She had a way with people – everyone loved her, you couldn't help it.

Certain times of day are worse than others - coming home, going to bed, lying on the couch, working on the computer, early morning. There is no squeaky toy noise. I miss it so.

Carolyn and I had planned a vacation trip to the beach for the week after Tutu's death. Carolyn, Priss, and I enjoyed it as best we could. It rained a lot - perhaps the beach missed Tutu also. Priss looked everywhere for her tiny, energetic friend, and she even did several things that she had never done before. Tutu always did them, but Tutu wasn't there this time. Priss walked along the tops of sofas and ate all her food and licked the bowl wanting more. Priss had never eaten all of her food since Carolyn brought her home. I wonder if Tutu's spirit is with her too.

PLAY PALS

Page 143

Shirley Hardee

Shirley was born and raised in Hampton, Virginia and attended Christopher Newport College. She raised five children and now has eight cherished grandchildren. She owned and operated the Oakcrest Riding School for 15 years. For the past 18 years she has been a real estate broker. She and husband Michael reside in Gloucester County where she enjoys playing golf, fishing, traveling, and playing various card and board games with friends. A life-time animal lover, she is now owned by a Papillon named Minnie.

Mending Heart Strings
by Shirley Hardee

My childhood memories always seem to include the joy and companionship of dogs. The early ones were mostly pets of one or another of my siblings, since I was the youngest of six children. These early dogs were all outside dogs, but when Mom and Dad were away, they managed an occasional visit inside.

Spot was the first special dog in my life. I found this little stray as a puppy and brought him home as my own. Mom insisted Spot stay outside, so he lived with my dad's numerous Beagles. He didn't seem to mind, because he was so happy that he had his own human. I felt just as happy having Spot as my own special companion. When I married, I took Spot with me.

Spot was followed by Sparky. A neighbor's German Shepherd whelped a litter of thirteen puppies and lacked sufficient milk to feed them all. So I brought Sparky home and hand raised him, feeding him every two hours during his first weeks of life. He grew to be a 110-pound devoted watchdog. Probably because of his size, he chose to live outside most of the time, enjoying the adventure and freedom of our 12-acre horse farm. He was never far from sight when any of my five children were outside at play.

Mickie eased into my life by degrees. She was a Pekinese who belonged to our neighbor. My son Jimmy often cared for her while the neighbor was away on trips. Mickie seemed to enjoy the visits, and soon began coming over to our house even when her owner was home. She seemed uninterested in returning to her own home and owner, finding Jimmy and the goings on at my house more entertaining. Her owner finally asked if we would like to adopt her formally, explaining that his work would require even more traveling in the future. He explained that he felt she already seemed to regard our home as hers and would run over to us any time he put her outside.

So Mickie came to stay. She immediately made it plain that her accommodations were inside with the children. But it was my feet that she followed all the time.

Mickie produced a litter of six puppies, from which we kept three including the smallest of the litter, a tri-color with a raccoon mask that we named Mitzie. This was the beginning of a wonderful bond between my dogs and me.

A few years later, Mitzie had a litter of three puppies. I kept the two little girls and gave the male who was named Buster to my mother.

The smaller of the girls was a tan-and-white female I named Sandy. At first Sandy attached herself to my middle child, a daughter named Mary Ellen. But when school began in the fall, and Mary Ellen went off to class, Sandy became my velcro child. My bed gradually became sleeping quarters for a gang of Pekinese with each one having their own special place on the bed. Weighing only six pounds and loving to cuddle, Sandy became my shadow and my traveling companion. She was often referred to as my real estate assistant.

Finally old age and various illnesses thinned the gang of Pekes around me. By her tenth birthday, Sandy was the only one left. It was very hard saying goodbye to these special pets in my life, and I was grateful to have Sandy to love. A little slow getting around and with eyesight beginning to fade, she still traveled with me whenever I could take her.

Then in 1991, my mother died, and Sandy's brother, Buster, came back to live with me and Sandy. He was friendly but never close to me like Sandy. He accepted our companionship up to a point, but he preferred not to sleep on the bed with us.

By March of 1995, Sandy was fifteen years old and almost blind. I carried her everywhere now, up and down stairs and in and out of the house. One morning I placed her in the yard for a few minutes, as I did several times a day, leaving her and Buster to take care of necessities while I went in the house to gather papers for a listing appointment I had scheduled for later in the morning. When I returned to bring her back inside a few minutes later, she had disappeared from the yard.

I searched everywhere for her to no avail. No one had seen her and I became more and more frantic. I called the humane society, the game warden, and local vets. Her vet suspected a hawk or owl had flown from a nearby wooded area and grabbed her.

Her disappearance and apparent tragic death left such a void in my heart, I vowed never to get another dog.

Mending Heart Strings

Buster and I went on after a fashion until his death a little over a year later, but my bed was empty and my heart seemed never to heal from the loss of Sandy. I had not been able to say goodbye and could never seem to find closure from the loss of my special little lady.

With Buster's death, I was without a companion dog for the first time in my life. Moreover, I felt that getting another one would betray the memory of Sandy. It took more than a few years, but when I finally decided to explore the possibility of another pet in my life. I knew I didn't want another Pekinese. I knew another would remind me too much of the pack of cherished Pekes that had been such a warm and comforting part of my life, especially Sandy. After much contemplation of what other type of dog would be best for me, I decided I wanted a Papillon. Right! Just after a little charmer called Kirby won Best in Show at Westminister. Just after the breed became nearly impossible to find.

Real estate brokers have to be persistent souls, however, and I persisted in my search for a breeder. When I found a local one, she shared a great deal of information about the breed and invited me to visit her kennel to interact with her gang of Papillons. During one of my visits she asked if I would like to adopt an older Papillon. She explained that the older dog would be a nice companion for me at the time, and would also be a companion for any future puppy I might get. I thought about the proposal and was back in a few days, ready to give the adoption a try.

And thus began my training as a companion to a butterfly dog.

Her name was Minerva or Minnie Mouse. She was eight years old when we met, a little shy and wary because she was not near the top of the pecking order at her old home. In fact, her elderly mother-in-law called the shots and Minnie was expected to take third billing after that elderly canine and her mate's older sister in her previous home. But

Minnie was very determined to let me know just what she wanted. Through facial expressions, eye movements and actions, she managed to get her message across very clearly.

She happily took over duties as real estate assistant. Her terms of employment were a bit more demanding than Sandy's had been, however. She didn't like being left in the car while I photographed the backs of properties, even when the air conditioning was left running. So she learned to turn off the AC which always brought me running.

She learned early that the buttons on the car door would roll down the glass and took to opening a window for herself while the car was cruising at 55 mph down Route 17. I rediscovered and learned always to employ the childproof controls on locks before setting out with her in the car.

She disliked sitting or lying in sunlight, so she always wanted a towel or throw in the car to crawl under to retreat from the sun. The first time I opened the small pass-through door from the back seat to the trunk in her presence, she concluded it was a doggie door to her new traveling condo. It now stays open all the time so she can climb back in the trunk and rest whenever she wishes as I drive.

Her new soft-sided carrier was greeted with eager acceptance. She jumped in and would lie quietly while I carried her in and around shopping malls.

I think I should carry a sign that reads "New Owner In Training" since she seems to be the one doing the teaching. I know for certain that her love and devotion is helping me repair the broken heart strings from the loss of Sandy. I know that Minnie and those that come after her will help to keep the heart strings going for a long time to come. Companions and teachers, they make life better for us all.

Jean C. Keating

Jean Keating holds degrees in Mathematics, Physics and Information Systems. As an aeronautical engineer with NASA and later Research Coordinator for Virginia's higher education coordinating board, she authored more than 50 scientific and data management reports and studies. She retired in 1998 and published her first work of fiction in September of 1999, a mystery set in Williamsburg and Richmond entitled *Amorous Accident*. She lives in Williamsburg, Virginia with 12 Papillons, one Chihuahua, two mixed-breed rescues, and two cats.

The Beginning After the End
by Jean C. Keating

Divorce after 19 years of marriage brought an abrupt end to life as I knew it and threw me, alone and bruised, into an unknown future. Faced with such events, men often buy sports cars they think they need. Women burden their financial situation with expensive purchases like diamond earrings which they never wear. Both sexes often enter into long-term job security arrangement with a shrink or two, just to have someone who will listen to their troubles.

Smugly, I decided not to fall into such weak-minded traps. Instead, I bought a show dog. I reasoned that a dog would give me the feeling of family and that showing a dog would be a hobby in which I could engage without benefit of a partner. Except for the dog, of course. Besides, I figured the dog would listen better than a shrink, and I wouldn't have to wait for an appointment either.

My father often told me that God looks after fools and drunks. I don't think my addiction to Coca-Cola counts as a drunk, so that leaves *fool*. As it turned out, I'd have spent less in the long run if I'd bought a bunch of sport cars in different colors to match my outfits and agreed to supporting a shrink for life. But it wouldn't have been nearly as satisfying.

With blissful ignorance, I persisted in my efforts to carve out a new arena of fun as a single and went off to some local dog shows. At my second show, I spotted the breed with whom I decided I wanted to share the rest of my now-single life. With total disregard and ignorance for the difficulty in getting a show-quality, Papillon bitch, I determinedly called the breeder of the dog I'd just met. Probably because the breeders were wonderful, caring people and read the good intentions behind the impetuousness, I soon became the proud and willing servant of a gorgeous black-and-white darling named Debonair Maaca Choice. Her father sired over 37 champions before I lost count. He was a Sire of Distinction many times over. Her mother had whelped 10 champions before Maaca and was a Dam of Distinction. It showed in their daughter's proud carriage and confident walk. I was humbly appreciative that she'd consider me as her companion.

The breeder warned me that Maaca 'sang' rather than barked. Of course, I didn't listen at the time, being far too busy marveling that this delightfully, self-assured little package was really going to join my life. Four weeks later, at the opening of a show in the Tar Heel Circuit, I got my first experience with what the breeder had tried to explain.

Pawprints on My Heart

Papillons were shown first one morning, so Maaca was there in the arms of her handler's father while the show opened with taped music of the National Anthem. Everyone else went silent, except Maaca, who proceeded to scream at the top of her lungs through the entire musical rendition. What her 'singing' lacked in tone and rhythm, she made up for in enthusiasm and volume.

It didn't take me long to determine that another Papillon trait was assertiveness. At a second show that weekend, I carried Maaca's crate to ringside (a no-no already), then opened it and invited her out in preparation for putting a lead around her neck. A group of Airedale terriers were getting ready to enter the ring just behind her crate. One handler saw his chance to demonstrate his entry's 'terrier-like qualities' by pointing his dog toward Maaca and instigating his dog's charge at my tiny friend. Bad move for both handler and Airedale. The handler meant to impress the judge in the Airedale ring......and he did, but not in the positive way he intended. First off, he picked the wrong toy on whom to try the stunt. Instead of cowering from the larger dog, Maaca let out a scream that could be heard in the next state and charged the Airedale. With hands that acted more from accident than design, I grabbed and held her while she struggled to reach the Airedale. She screamed her defiance of him and his handler, and probably hurled insults at his ancestors going all the way back to the beginning of time. The vet came running from six rings away, convinced that a dog had been fatally hurt. The Airedale cringed behind his handler, and I was evil enough to note later that the offending handler and his charge placed dead last in their class.

And if you believe elephants are the only animals that never forget, you never met my Maaca. To the end of her days, she would start screaming anytime she saw an Airedale. I guess she was still determined to continue the blood-feud with any possible ancestors or descendants of her original nemesis.

Between attending classes to learn how to hold Maaca's lead properly and practicing how to walk around the show ring without stumbling over my own two feet, my nights were fully occupied. Weekends flew by with pre-dawn risings to drive to dog shows, all of which seem to be in neighboring states or down roads that weren't properly labeled on my map. I was too busy being a willing servant to the royal one to miss another human at the dinner table. My companion listened quietly to all my troubles, sang a bit in sympathy, and never sent me a bill for the services.

I quickly learned that she carried in her genes more knowledge of dog shows than I would ever acquire. Our first two shows were successful only because she nearly tripped me to get me out of the line of sight between her exalted self and the judge's eyes. I finally took the hint, took the coward's way out, and hired a professional handler to accompany her into the ring. I retired to a chair at ring-side from which I could marvel at her performance.

She could tell the judge from the steward before she got within 10 feet of the entrance to a show ring. Goo-goo eyes and butterfly-ear waves were reserved for judges. Ring stewards might stand over, handle, and monitor the ribbons, but they handed them to the judges who decided the winners. I never once saw Maaca waste a glance on a steward. Somewhere in her DNA resided the ability to tell who was judge and who was steward along with the reasoning that only judges awarded the treasured ribbon. She was an AKC conformation champion within five weeks.

Of course, all these travel costs, show entries, and handler's fees didn't come cheap. About the cost of a quarter of my pink sports car, I would estimate.

But life was fun. So we decided, Maaca and I, to make it even more fun with the addition of some little Maacas. Naturally only a mate several states away would do, which meant more expense for travel and dowry (otherwise known as stud fee) . And our precious little puppies couldn't be whelped or begin life anywhere but in a baby play pen with matching blankets, comforter, puddle pads, receiving blankets, and toys. I began to suspect that I was somewhat strange when my vet remarked that his two sons had less baby stuff than my first litter and moreover, none of his children's stuff matched. But, says I, don't all babies need a complete set of Winnie-the-Pooh including a large stuffed Pooh-Bear with which to sleep? I had to concede the point that I might have gone a bit overboard when my accountant remarked that I could have bought the other three-quarters of my sports car for the money I'd spent in vet bills, nursery fixtures, and supplies and food supplements.

So, my dad was right. God looks after fools in spite of themselves. Oh, I could have had the sports car, but it would have grown old and rusty. With my choice, I never lacked for a listener, or someone to share my joys or sad times, no appointments necessary. It was hard to remain down, no matter how bad the day, with active little fur-people dancing around, wanting to be petted, kissing my ears, or licking my face. And their comic races around the house at hearing me laugh intensified the happy times even more. I returned home each night to one or more happy, wiggling bodies in my entrance way, dancing on back legs and pawing the air in joy at my return. The house was filled with the warmth of love along with the occasional dog hair in my soup.

And Maaca gave me Mischief who gave me Bear who gave me Imp who gave me.....well, you get the picture. Some things in life are worth a lot more than an entire stable of sport cars!

A Dog By Any Other Name
by Jean C. Keating

He was the tiniest, youngest living thing I'd ever seen when his dam dropped him, still in his sack, into my hand. I named him Mischief Maaca after his mother. I called him Mischief. No one told me then that I needed to exercise care in what I picked for a name. Maybe other breeds don't pay attention to what labels you put on them. I don't remember that the mixed-breeds I grew up loving seemed to care. But after twenty years of living with a delightful, willful, thinking breed called Papillon, I've come to believe these little butterfly dogs not only understand, they try to live up to their names.

But I didn't know that in 1983. And Mischief proceeded to live up to his name from the day his eyes opened.

Pawprints on My Heart

At ten days of age, one eye was slightly open, the other still sealed closed. Yet somehow he managed to squirm up over the bolster padding lining the play pen, find a microscopic break in the netting--in a new playpen, mind you--and push his equally tiny head through the net.

As he grew older my efforts to train him to a lead were met with attempts to leap up and bite me on my backside.

Any surface set to confine him was a challenge to be climbed, scaled, or penetrated. Even X-pens had to have tops to contain him. If he was confined to a crate, he amused himself with practicing coyote howls. Baby gates were delightful challenges. He ate through them if they were plastic webbing or wooden uprights. If net and plastic were replaced with metal sheets, he scaled them. I tried a regular baby gate on the top of a modified one with metal sheets for sections. He climbed the lower gate and chewed through the upper one's mesh while balancing himself on the edge of the lower gate.

He loved carrying things in his mouth. His two favorites were an orange plastic crab with squeaker and a large stuffed figure I called Green Dragon. The latter was a stuffed green dinosaur that was almost as big as he. Fortunately, he didn't like to hear the squeaker and didn't try to remove it from his crab. But he loved to shake and play tug with Green Dragon, producing chunks of stuffing. Repair work was done with whatever color of stuffing was available, so succeeding accidents resulted in multi-colored stuffing dotting floors, sofa, chairs, and my bed. After frequent repairs and washings, I attempted to throw the stained and battered toy away. Mischief always seemed to find it, however, and would appear at the door on my return home at night with the prized hunk again in his mouth. I think he made a pact with the housekeeper to retrieve it from the depths of the trash where I'd thrown it.

By six months, he could grasp his metal dish by the side and sling it around to empty it of any contents he didn't find appealing or bang it against my feet to get more or different food.

He decided early on that azaleas didn't belong in pots on the back deck, so he'd simply prune out of existence whatever I planted.

I had been warned that Papillons took seriously their role as companion dogs. I actually enjoyed having a velcro dog and being followed everywhere around the house. But I did think it was acceptable to take a bath and read in the tub as long as he was allowed access to guard me from the rug on the bathroom floor. I was wrong! One night I got too engrossed in a mystery and ended up with 3.5 pounds of dog poised on 16 tiny toenails pressed into my bare stomach. You don't even want to know what the pounds per square inch works out to be in that scenario The book ended up in the water and I never did learn how it ended.

It was hard to scold the little minx, however. When called, he'd come at a gallop only to stop in front of me, rise on his back legs, and stretch his front legs to be picked up. In my arms, he'd place little paws on either side of my head and rain doggie kisses on my face and ears, before settling down with his muzzle tucked under my chin.

Early in his second year, a business trip took me away for a week and I imposed on two friends to come over twice each day to feed, water and exercise the growing pack of dogs I now called the Astra gang. The other members of the pack were very well behaved, but Mischief pawed the front door open and ran out and down the street, trailed by the frantic Registrar and Associate Provost of the College of William and Mary. The latter never really forgave him for causing her to lose her dignity to the point of screaming after him as he raced toward the traffic on Williamsburg's main street.

As the years rolled by for both of us, his methods of shadowing and guarding changed. I got up more frequently at night and he was less and less active about following. At about eight, he began to get up and reposition himself at the end of the bed rather than following me. I imagined his conversation. "I can tell from here that there are no bad-things there. So I'll just wait here."

As more time passed and I got up more than once, a little bit of complaining seemed to creep into his imagined conversation. "You really have to turn the light on? Again? How can I get any sleep with you turning on the light all the time?"

In his final years, his hearing was bad so he adopted another approach to make certain he would awaken when I did. He repositioned his sleeping place between me and the edge of the bed, pinning the covers down on me so that I could no longer get up without moving him aside. No amount of pleading or moving him before I went to sleep, would do any good. He'd always shift his position after I was asleep and I'd find his softly snoring body between me and the edge of the bed upon attempting to arise later in the night.

When Hurricane Hugo went through in 1989, two little kittens were left homeless and came to join the Astra pack. Never having lived with a feline before, I raised them as I would any puppy. The little female was no problem, staying on top of my desk or the back of a sofa most of the time and basically ignoring the twelve or so canines that populated the house at the time of her arrival. The male cat Sunny quickly became the bane of Mischief's existence.

To all canines except Mischief, Sunny was friend and playmate. He played happily with Mischief's brother Rusty. Rusty would chase Sunny awhile, and then Sunny would chase Rusty. Sunny even assumed puppy-sitting chores when mother dogs went outside, curling around nursing puppies and keeping them warm. Forever etched on my brain cells is the startled look on Sunny's face one day when one puppy with nearly four-week old teeth decided to nurse him. To his credit, he gave a cat's version of a grimace, pushed the offending puppy away, but did not abandon his charges until the mother returned to resume her duties in the puppy pen. But Mischief and Sunny were always adversaries. Mischief wanted to boss and herd Sunny, and Sunny wouldn't cooperate.

Sunny grew to 18 pounds with back and legs that were twice the length of the pugnacious little dog's. Mischief would charge the larger animal, barking and fussing. Sunny never hissed or tried to use his claws. He would simply turn a shoulder to the little dog and bump him aside. It was laughable until it happened in the upstairs hallway and the bump hurtled Mischief through the banisters and into the entrance way below.

I was coming down the upstairs hallway and saw it happen, but it was over and done too swiftly for me to do anything. I heard one yelp from Mischief as the little body went flying through space. I rushed downstairs expecting to find his broken body on the first floor. Instead, a puzzled little fellow looked up and whined, then stood up on his hind legs, front paws raised toward me to pick him up in my arms. He coughed when I finally settled him gingerly in my arms, so I quickly alerted every emergency vet I could find. Mischief was, after all, three months short of his 15th birthday. The emergency team could find nothing wrong--no concussion, no broken or cracked legs or ribs, no sign of internal trauma. His own vet could find nothing wrong the next day either, except a lot of sore muscles. Two days later, Mischief was back trying to boss and herd the cat, having learned nothing from his fall.

Despite his tiny size--barely six pounds at his top weight--Mischief was determined to rule his own turf and any remaining ground within his sight or hearing. The nightly walk down the center of our street by my neighbor and his Shar-pei was a challenge to Mischief's authority, at least in his own mind, and was met with loud barking and jumping against the fence around our yard. One evening, Mischief's rowdy pushing succeeded in dislodging the latch on the gate, and he was through the tiny break in the enclosure and after the hated Shar-pei with me in hot pursuit. Of course, I was considerably heavier and slower, so Mischief reached the Shar-pei first with disastrous results. The Shar-pei pulled his master down in the street trying to reach the little red-and-white attacker, and succeeded in grabbing Mischief across the back and shaking him. My neighbor managed to get up and beat his dog over his head with the plastic handle of his retractable leash until the bigger dog released my tiny combatant. When I finally arrived on the scene, my subdued tyrant stumbled toward me whimpering, too shaken to stand on his hind legs. I exchanged necessary apologies with my neighbor, and rushed home with Mischief in my arms to examine his many bleeding wounds. I determined that the grip achieved by the Shar-pei had been off center and not placed to achieve the larger dog's objective--to crush the rib cage and kill his small foe. But there were many oozing puncture wounds and much tearing of surface skin and muscle around the marks of the fangs.

It was late evening. I was certain that if I called my own vet he would want to keep Mischief overnight. I was equally certain I didn't want to leave him alone. So I checked for shock and read up on shock formulas. Unfortunately, the four tablespoons of rock candy soaked in brandy wasn't in my medicine chest, so I improvised. All that night, I held and rocked a little dog, while administering sixty proof Hiram Walker Orange Curacao, checking gums for any paleness that would indicate a level of shock that would require seeking professional help, and changing compresses to his seeping wounds. We arrived at our regular vet's when he opened the next morning. Mischief was crocked but otherwise the same, I was numb from lack of sleep, and my vet asked to see my reference book so he could read up and be forewarned of any other startling remedies I might unwisely choose to try in the future.

This fracas left Mischief with bad injuries to his skin which took months to heal. The hair which was shaved from around the puncture wounds was very slow to regrow, so summer and winter for two years, he changed as many as three times a day into different little short-sleeved shirts that covered his hairless areas and protected him from the chill of the air conditioning in summer and from the cooler temperatures of winter. He enjoyed the attention from me and from others because of his little shirts and was always eager and cooperative when asked to "change his shirt."

For the last year of Mischief's life, I was fortunate to retire and spend my days at home with him. When he began to suffer from seizures just past his sixteenth birthday, I made certain his medication was packed along with my keys and license. Where I went, he went also. He continued to amaze me with his intelligent adjustment to life and his spunk. When I'd whisper "medicine" in his ear, he'd bravely open his mouth, roll back his lips, and remain still while I smeared a mixture of crushed medicine in Nutri-Cal on the roof of his mouth, then close and swallow the sticky mixture without a fuss. But he continued to try to herd the cat and keep the other members of the pack in line, herding them outside and back inside as he thought they should go.

To the end of his days, he lived up to his name of Mischief Maaca. And he's not the only pap I've known that seemed to take his cue from the name he was given. Consider the two dogs whose histories follow.

Nana Ridgeway whelped a seven ounce puppy on July 7, 1997. She named him Magnificent Seven. He was assigned the number seven in each of the shows in which he was entered. He was his dam's seventh puppy, and finished his championship in seven months. And he was Nanken Papillons' seventh Champion. Of course, she called him Seven.

Lou Ann King named a young puppy Lotiki's Supernatural Being. He went on to win the triple crown of dogdom. No other dog in the history of showing has achieved wins of Best in Show at the World Show, the Royal International Show, and at Westminister Kennel Club. Dog lovers around the world know of and love the beautiful showman many remember only as Kirby.

I don't know if my beloved Mischief would have avoided some of his bad scrapes and perhaps lived with me longer if I'd named him something quieter. I sometimes think I can see him still, just past the limits of my peripheral vision. If I reach down, without looking, I can stroke an elegant head and compact body beneath silken fur that seems very familiar. If I don't caress the ears, I can fool myself that the body I touch is Mischief's. But the larger ears and fuller fringes are a tactile clue that I touch Mischief's son. And the cat curled next to him is another indication that the body which stretches to press its head higher into the palm of my hand is not Sunny's old nemesis. I gave this one a calmer name, Astra's Hardly Holy. So far, in fourteen years, he's never been in a fight or gotten injured. I've tried to make certain that his life would run smoothly. I've called him Holy.

Who's In Charge Here?
by Jean C. Keating

The Papillons of today are descendants of the dwarf continental spaniels of the French royal courts in the 15th century. Tiny, light-boned, and ever ready to get into pranks, they are a never ending source of enjoyment and wonder. They also have tremendous strength of will and they never forget that they descend from royalty. The word imperious often comes to mind and conversation when discussing these elegant little fur-people.

My first Papillon took over my life two months before her first birthday. Her full name was Debonair Maaca Choice.

Pawprints on My Heart

Within five weeks, she added the title Champion to the front of her name by prancing herself to wins at numerous dogs shows. Her method was to march in the ring, look the judge right in the eye, and say very plainly in body language, "I'm here. I'm the best. I want the ribbon, so send the rest of these also-rans home!"

By two years of age, she'd taken over my bed, produced two sons to carry on her legacy, and managed to keep us all in line without the slightest matting of her silky black-and-white coat. She was a lady and a queen. You could almost hear her talking in the royal first person plural.

Her second-born son was named Mischief Maaca. From the moment his eyes and ears opened, he proceeded to live up to his name. He was all the things his royal dam was not - loud, brash, and vocally assertive. He appeared to boss everyone around and the remainder of the pack usually gave him his way. The Queen was always nearby – with a look that conveyed, "We are not amused at anyone or anything that upsets the Prince!"

Mischief was almost two years old when friends came to visit bringing along their nine-month old Scottish terrier, Malcolm. As my human visitors and I stood around in the living room discussing afternoon events and evening dinner arrangements, the Papillon pack and one immature Scottie milled around on the floor at our feet. Malcolm spotted a chew stick on the floor that looked appealing and moved toward it. Mischief immediately rushed to defend the chewie with loud growling and posturing. Scotties seem to process information at a much slower rate than the lightening-quick Paps, but Malcolm was steady in his advancement against the posturing Mischief. Human conversation refocused on the contest of wills exhibited between Pap and Scottie. Malcolm's steady advance was met with increasingly loud grumbles and growls from Mischief, but in the face of an adversary that outweighed him 16 pounds to 5 pounds, Mischief retreated to continue his fussing from the safe position behind my legs. Satisfied at last that he understood the lay-of-the land, Malcolm claimed his chew stick and settled down on the rug to enjoy his prize, facing the vocalizing Papillon. I was not concerned with 'family honor,' but did want to insure that my young Pap's continual growling did not escalate into physical contact in which one of the two young dogs might be hurt....the one injured most likely to be my smaller fur-child. I made certain both were on leashes and returned to discussing dinner plans with my human guests.

The Queen had other ideas. Out of the corner of my eye, I noted her quiet but confident approach to within three feet of the Scottie. Making certain she had his attention, she settled gracefully on the rug and began to chew on another rawhide stick she'd brought with her. To my guests, this meant nothing. The toy box in the corner of the great room was loaded with toys and chew sticks. But I noted the oddity; this was the first time I had ever known the Queen to bother with toys or chew sticks. She expected them to be offered with her dinner tray but never went looking for them otherwise.

The Scottie chewed more slowly on his recently acquired trophy as he focused more and more on the one being enjoyed by the Queen. Entrapment might not be a word the Queen understood, but she obviously understood the concept and how to apply it effectively. Finally Malcolm abandoned his prize all together, and arose to check out the one being enjoyed by the quiet, black-and white dog in front of him. He approached confidently to within a head length of her muzzle before his advance was finally arrested by a low, soft growl from the Queen.

The Scottie's thought processes could be read as if a movie was running in slow motion. He stopped and looked pointedly at the Queen. She returned to quietly chewing her toy. He took a step toward her, only to be stopped by a second, low, warning growl. He looked back at Mischief who still fussed loudly – from a safe distance behind my legs. Malcolm looked at the chew toy he'd contested with Mischief and won. He looked again at the calm lady dog in front of him. "Ah. No problem," he appeared to reason. "All that posturing and the other one backed off. No problem with this quieter one." So Malcolm grabbed for the chewie in the Queen's mouth.

Quick as a rattlesnake's strike, the Queen dropped her chewie, nailed him with a full mouth of teeth across his long, reaching muzzle, and administered another growl that only an experienced mother dog can deliver. Then before he could shake his head she'd retrieved her prize, returned to her prone position and resumed chewing her rawhide stick.

I couldn't help it. I laughed aloud at the poor Scottie youngster. He shook his head in disbelief. He looked at Mischief, still growling at him, but doing nothing. He looked at the Queen, calmly chewing on her prize and making not a sound. He shook his smarting muzzle and finally sought the comfort of his owner's side, still puzzled by the conflicting signals he'd read. But I'd guess that next time he'll spend a bit more time figuring out just where the power really lies in dog packs.

His brief visit with the Queen and her heir-apparent hopefully taught him the difference between real control and the noisy behavior of a "wannabe." I hope he grew, in time, to appreciate her teaching. After all, anything I needed to know about group dynamics I learned from my Papillons.

Winter Wonder
by Jean C. Keating

The first month of the new century brought the deepest accumulation of snow in a decade. All day, fragile flakes of white piled up on ground and outdoor structures. Filigreed fluff turned to liquid upon contact with my hands, but clung tenaciously to everything else. An ever-growing depth of white padding quickly covered my succeeding attempts to provide bird seed to a frustrated feathered mob. An active breeze kept snow from building up on power lines, and whipped the falling flakes into drifts that reached 15 inches in depth. In Maine, this might not have counted for much of a snow fall. In Williamsburg, Virginia this qualified as a blizzard.

It was a wonderful opportunity for writing. My canine fur-children, collectively known as the Astra gang, had no interest in going out after their encounters with the first four inches of the squishy stuff. And I certainly wasn't going to drive in the mess. Besides, I was two months behind on my book. Logical arguments aside, I failed at any productive effort. I frittered away the day, enjoying nature's beauty but creating none on my own. It was after nine in the evening when I realized HE had entered my life.

His dam finished her championship last year, but this was her first litter. An x-ray the previous day had found two puppies. I expected their arrival in two days, to coincide with the 63rd day from the first mating. The small, four-ounce male didn't wait. His soft squeaks charged my energy banks and brought me to the whelping box quickly. I sat transfixed at the sight of his tiny body, wide white blaze and nose band. I marveled aloud to dam and pup at the resemblance of this wee mite to his great-grandfather, my constant shadow for 16.5 years. Like the snow which still fell softly outside, he was fragile but resolute. He crawled vigorously to join with his mother for support and sustenance.

Two days later he was still trying to nurse but losing ground. Patient and tenacious, he clung to life. I marshaled friends with four-wheel drive to take mother and baby to the vet through piles of snow that thwarted efforts to clear roads and parking lots. His mother's milk was insufficient, but substitutes were feebly rejected by a tiny paw he attempted to put between my feeder and his mouth. The snow which preceded his birth clung to the landscape as determinedly as he did to life. Through the weeks to come, we battled swollen lymph glands and a reluctant appetite.

Winter Wonder

After a week, the lymph glands returned to normal and he gained to 5 ounces. I cautiously named him in keeping with Astra Kennel conventions. His was the 'W' litter so he became Astra's Winter Wonder. It seemed fitting considering the piles of snow that still covered everything. Of course, he needed a call-name also, so I dubbed him Shadow after his beloved great-grandfather.

My Winter Wonder, my Shadow, had to be supplemented every two hours, and I watched the wonder of life unfolding within my hands. He grew from the 3.5 ounces at two days to a fluffy bundle of 16 ounces. Each half-ounce gain was recorded and greeted with joy and celebration, as ear flaps unsealed and tiny eyes opened to deep blue pools of curiosity. His little paw still sought to plant itself between his mouth and my eyedropper of milk supplement, however. He wanted his mother's milk, but he couldn't compete with his larger sister who got most of his mother's limited supply and licked his face clean of any extra supplements that missed his mouth.

I carried him in my hand and against my shoulder or tucked him into a sleeping ring with hot water bottles so that he slept inches away from the keyboard on my desk. I would talk to him about the quiet scene of white outside, the strength of the tiny snowflakes that clung to landscape and structures despite temperatures that reached into the mid-40's during the day, and all the reasons I never seemed to be tenacious about my writing. "I have this rental house, Shadow, and it takes up so much of my time that I don't have time to write." He'd gaze steadily at me with his dark blue eyes and yawn. Or, "I really have to finish my taxes before I can concentrate on trying to write." Another yawn.

By four weeks he was bopping around on the floor of the playpen he shared with his sister and dam, and learning to manipulate me, a Papillon's favorite chore. He'd run between his crate and the wall of his play pen until he couldn't go forward any more. Then he'd whine and look at me to move the crate. As long as I stayed within his view, he'd whine for my help. If I left the room to watch him from hiding, he'd easily reverse his path back to his play or sleeping area.

He still spent many hours on my desk, yawning at my excuses. Between feedings and petting sessions, I managed to deal with putting the rental property on the market. It sold the next day.

Just before his fifth week of life, his breathing became more rapid. As usual, he fought against any of my food offerings, that same dainty paw always raised to push away the baby food or puppy mush I forced upon him. His vets were very guarded, suggesting that his lungs were not functioning properly and might indicate pneumonia. He lost interest in playing and spent more and more time within the warm circle of water bottles in his sleeping ring on my desk. We went back to two-hour feedings and brief outings of walking around the surface of my desk. He'd sleep for brief spaces of time as long as I remained near. There was no excuse for not working on taxes while I waited for him to nap before accepting more water and food supplements.

He'd stretch and whine when he wanted attention, and I'd often give him an update of the completion of this or that part of the tax information. He'd push his little pillow (shaped like a dog bone) into a more comfortable position and go back to sleep.

On his 40th day of life, I finished compiling my tax information and put it into a folder to take to my accountant. The minute I finished, Shadow opened those beautifully expressive blue eyes, gathered himself up and jumped out of his sleeping ring directly into my hands. Suddenly he seemed too weak to stand or to hold up his head. I caressed him gently and tucked him under my chin.

Winter Wonder

That tiny paw patted my chin one last time and he was gone, softly and quietly, like the snow that fell the night of his birth.

That snow is long gone now except for the lasting memories that exist in photographs and stories of Williamsburg's blizzard. Winter Wonder's brief passage through my life is over too; only a few photographs and his story remain.

Like the great-grandfather he resembled so much, he'd reminded me that tenacity and quiet strength can accomplish almost anything. He'd done his job in only 40 days, returned my efforts to writing the story of the Astra gang, and caused me to wonder. Did the spirit of his beloved ancestor come back in this tiny body to touch my life again, to remind me that I have things to do before I join them all at Rainbow Bridge?

Day's End
by Jean C. Keating

The day has been cooler and dryer than most June eighths in Tidewater Virginia. It's a beautiful evening to be outside with "the children," and a special day of thanksgiving here in the Astra digs.

Fifteen small dogs, collectively called the Astra pack, play or rest on or near me in our back yard. Four generations of Papillons carrying the Astra prefix mingle with several rescue Chihuahuas. Fallon, the oldest, celebrated her 16th birthday today. That's about 90 in human years, so she's even older now than I. Each day with an old dog is a victory, but this birthday is more precious than most.

A year ago tonight, Fallon's long-time mate and bed partner and my constant shadow for sixteen plus years went into cluster seizures. He died the next day. Mischief was 18 months old when Fallon came to us as a three-month-old puppy, and he was always at her side through all her near-fifteen years. Her grief at his death was as deep and debilitating as mine. She refused to eat for four days and I thought I'd lose her too, but she rallied in response to my pleas not to leave me. So this birthday celebration has been especially prized, because I was certain we would never be together on this day.

High intensity lights from the adjacent parking lot of William and Mary Hall filter through the foliage of trees covering the deep stretch of woods in back. The wavering streamers of light turn the white on the "fur-children's" bodies to silver. Evening colors shift from that special grey-blue shot with mauve that is navigational twilight into the deep inky blackness of astronomical twilight and beyond. Fireflies create brief sparks of light in the yard. Two five-month old puppies, Fallon's great-great grandchildren, dart to and fro trying to catch the points of light, tumbling into each other and their older relatives who amble about or lie quietly in the grass.

Earlier Fallon and I went to Taco Bell for her yearly treat of a taco. Health problems dictate that tonight's treat is but a tiny pinch of the spicy meat mixture, but her old nose and taste buds still enjoy the adventure. She licks an imagined trace of it off her nose as she sits on the steps of the deck, a padded dog bed between her bony body and the rough wood. She leans against me to rest. Any slight break from her routine of sleeping away the day is a strain now.

The wolf sable markings and heavy fringes of Fallon's youth are grey and thinning. Up close, the lines of

Pawprints on My Heart

the wide blaze and noseband can be discerned from the dirty white of the greying wolf-sable coat. In the dim light of evening, the head which rests trustingly and contentedly in my hand looks almost solid white except for dark eye rims and black fringed ears.

The younger of the puppies darts over to say hello, rises on dancing back legs to paw rapidly with flying front feet at my knees and Fallon's face. My old friend grumbles softly and jerks her head out of the way of the over-active leprechaun that is a Papillon puppy of six months. I gently divert the flying puppy paws and redirect the energy by throwing a toy for my youngest fur-child to retrieve. Afraid of missing out on something, Fallon's son Holy uncurls himself from my White Christmas hosta, which he regards as his personal outdoor bed, and ambles over for an ear scratch.

One of the rescues resembles a small Jack Russell terrier. The explosive energy of the terrier shows now in another burst of chases and tumbles with the two young Papillons.

Soon even the small terrier and the puppies will finish their play, and we'll all go inside for dinner and a little TV. Food, water, and medication needed by some of the ancient ones are ready in each of their sleeping crates, along with fresh soft pads and little blankets to be crunched into pillows according to the taste of each canine. Friends and my vet laughingly call my home the geriatric ward for small dogs. Fallon is now 16; Happy and Holy are fourteen going on fifteen; Ivory, Imp and Pixie are over thirteen. We've been together a long time in dog years, but it is never long enough.

Divorced and childless, I once worried that I would grow old alone, without the warmth of a family circle. Now I know the family is here, the spirits and coverings of them changing, shifting with the years, but always near, always supportive, always ready to lick my tears away or bark and leap with joy at my laughter

Day's End

Today has had its ups and downs, like most normal days. Day's end finds us comfortable with and comforted by each other. Most of all, we're grateful at the victory over time and aging that has given us another day together.